They had taken Dora in today as if she had never left after last summer.

They treated her like one of them. An old friend. No different than anyone, not even the town's Top Dawg: Burke Burdette.

To be treated like one of the crowd had to drive a man like Burke, a man who defined himself by his position, his accomplishments, his respect as a leader, crazy.

Dora smiled to herself. Mt. Knott might drive Burke crazy, but she was just crazy about the place, and the people. She couldn't think of a nicer, warmer, sweeter place to be during the Christmas season, and she looked forward to the town-wide event tomorrow night.

Burke hadn't wanted her to stay for Mt. Knott's Christmas kickoff. He'd asked her to come here, but now he did not want her to stay. Why?

If it were possible, she felt even more unwanted by Burke now than she had sitting alone in her office the day after Thanksgiving. What had she gotten herself into? And how did she get out?

ANNIE JONES

Winner of the Holt Medallion for Southern Themed Fiction, and the *Houston Chronicle*'s Best Christian Fiction Author of 1999, Annie Jones grew up in a family that loved to laugh, eat and talk—often all at the same time. They instilled in her the gift of sharing through words and humor, and the confidence to go after her heart's desire (and to act fast if she wanted the last chicken leg). A former social worker, she feels called to be a "voice for the voiceless" and has carried that calling into her writing by creating characters often overlooked in our fast-paced culture—from seventy-somethings who still have a zest for life to women over thirty with big mouths and hearts to match. Having moved thirteen times during her marriage, she is currently living in rural Kentucky with her husband and two children.

Somebody's Santa
Annie Jones

Steeple
Hill®

Published by Steeple Hill Books™

STEEPLE HILL BOOKS

Steeple
Hill®

ISBN-13: 978-0-373-81377-3
ISBN-10:   0-373-81377-5

SOMEBODY'S SANTA

She will give birth to a son, and you are to give him the name Jesus, because he will save his people from their sins.

—*Matthew* 1:21

To my family far and wide (yeah, the older we get the wider we are!): For all the merry Christmases past and all the joyous new years to come, thank you and God bless!

Chapter One

Burke Burdett had lost himself.

The man he had always believed himself to be had vanished. Nobody needed him anymore. Nobody wanted him. Nobody even realized that he had gone.

It had happened so quickly he still didn't know where he fit into the grand scheme of his company, his family or even his own life. But he did know this—years ago he had made a promise and now he had to see that promise through, even if it meant he had to go someplace he swore he'd never go to ask help of someone he swore he'd never see again. Even if it meant that he had to trade in his image of Top Dawg, the eldest and leader of the pack of Burdett brothers, to become somebody that nobody in Mt. Knott, South Carolina, would ever have imagined. If Burke ever hoped to find himself again, he was going to have to become Santa Claus.

Fat, wet snowflakes powdered the gray-white Carolina sky. Dried stalks of grass and weeds poked through the threadbare blanket of white. Everything seemed swathed in peace and quiet solitude.

Winter weather was not unheard of in this part of South Carolina, but Burke Burdett had rarely seen it come this early in the year, nor had he ever considered it the answer to somebody's prayer. His prayer.

He looked to the heavens and muttered—mostly to himself but not caring if the God of all creation, maker of the sky, and mountains and gentle nudges in the form of frozen precipitation, overheard—" And on Thanksgiving Day of all times."

It had to be Thanksgiving, of course, one of the few days when Burke took the time to actually offer a prayer much beyond a mumbled appeal for help or guidance.

This time he had asked for a little of each and added to the mix a heartfelt plea, "Please, prepare my heart for what I am about to undertake. Give it meaning by giving me purpose."

If he were another kind of man, he could have waxed eloquent about love and honor and humbling himself in order to learn and grow from the experience. But he wasn't that kind of man. He was the kind of man who wanted to feel productive and useful. There were worse ambitions than asking to be useful to the Lord, he believed.

So he had left his prayer as it was and waited for something to stir in him. It had stirred outside instead. Snow. In November.

The whole family had ooohed and ahhhed over it, and for an instant, Burke recalled how it felt to be a kid. And just as quickly he excused himself and drove awry from the family compound of homes.

Now in the vacant parking lot of the old building that housed his family's business, the Carolina Crumble Pattie factory, Burke did not feel the cold. Only a dull, deepening sense of loneliness that had dogged him after spending a day surrounded by his family. In years past that family had consisted of his mom and dad, Conner and Maggie Burdett, his three brothers, Adam, Jason and Cody, and maybe a random cousin or two in from Charleston. This year two sisters-in-law and a nephew had been added. But it was the losses that Burke simply could not shake.

Age and grief had ravaged the tough old bird who had once been the strong, proud Conner Burdett, left him thin and a little stooped, worn around the eyes and unexpectedly sentimental.

Sentiment was not the Burdett way and seeing it in his father made Burke think of weakness and vulnerability. Not his father's but his own.

Burke clenched and unclenched his jaw and squinted at the low yellow-and-tan building where he had worked since he'd been old enough to ride his bicycle there after school. It did not help that the realities of the changing market had their business by the throat and had all but choked the life out of what had once been the mainstay of employment for much of the town of Mt. Knott, South Carolina.

They had made a plan to deal with that, or rather, his brother Adam had. He had gone out into the global marketplace, learned new techniques and made powerful allies. He was the one, the family had concluded by an almost unanimous vote, who needed to take the reins now. That plan had come at a cost. Burke, who had always carried the title Top Dawg in the pack of Burdett boys, had been asked to step aside.

Step aside or be forced out. By his own family.

In doing so Burke had lost his place not just in the family but, he thought, in the whole wide world. Not that they had fired him outright. They had asked him to stay on in a different capacity, but they must have known he'd never do it. After all, who had ever heard of Upper Middle Management Dawg?

So he had tendered his resignation and never returned, not even to collect his belongings. Until now.

Adam was to take on the job that Burke had held, for all intents and purposes, for a decade now. Adam, with his expertise in international corporate business dealings. Adam, with his new ideas for marketing and distribution. Adam, with the one thing that made him the most honored in the eyes of Conner Burdett, the thing that would assure them all that their name and reputation and even their business would go on—a son.

Burke didn't even have a girlfriend. How was he supposed to compete with that?

He wasn't, of course. To know that, Burke only had to think about Adam and Josie and their son, Nathan, how happy they had looked today seated at the massive Burdett dinner table together. Love and joy and wanting the best for those you care about, *doing* your best for them, that was what mattered. Winning?

Winning, Burke decided as he let out a long, labored sigh, was for losers.

And for the first time in his life, Burke felt like a loser. Not because of the loss of his position with the company or the unlikelihood that he would become a husband and father anytime soon, but because he had failed at that one thing that really mattered in life.

Burke shuddered. The wind whipped at the collar of his brown suede coat. He pushed his gray Stetson down low, as much to hide the dark blond hair that everyone in town would recognize as to protect his head and ears from the cold. Today, Thanksgiving Day, he felt the cutting ache of the loss of his mother down to his very bones. She had died two years ago, come Christmas Eve. *Two years.*

Yet it felt so fresh that he could still feel the heft of her coffin as he led the procession of pallbearers that day. He flexed his hand as if to chase away the memory of the icy brass handle he had clutched to take his mother to her final resting place. But it had been too long.

He had let too much time go past and now he had to face the truth.

Until this year the running of "the crumble," as everyone in Mt. Knott affectionately called the business, had kept him busy. It had occupied his time, his thoughts, his energy. He hadn't even had time for dating, much less a real relationship, for seeing friends or making a real home for himself or any of the niceties most people his age took for granted. He certainly didn't have time to take on some silly pet cause of his mother's. One he didn't understand, didn't approve of and had only learned about when she was on her deathbed. Even if it was the one thing she had asked that Burke and Burke alone, of all the brothers, undertake. Her dying wish.

He swiped a knuckle across his forehead to nudge back his hat, ignoring the sudden sting of a flake that swirled beneath his Stetson to land on his cheek.

His finger brushed over the faint old scar that jagged across his eyebrow.

Conner had given it to him—the scar, not the business. The Crumble he had had to fight for in every sense of the word. He'd used the law, his family's consensus and finally even his fists to win his birthright as oldest of the four Burdett sons. His birthright—his place as head of the Burdett household and CEO of the family's already foundering enterprise.

Burke had gotten that scar the night he'd taken over as head of the family business. He'd been running it behind the scenes while his mother was sick, without much input at all from the rest of the family, but Conner's name had always remained painted in gold on the glass of the door to the big office. Until that night. That night everything had shifted, like a great jutting up of land along a fault line. They had all known it would come one day but had done little to prepare for it.

That night Adam had cashed out his share

of the Crumble factory, taken the inheritance his mother had left and run away. And Conner and Burke had pushed their always contentious relationship to the edge.

He hung his head. Even after all these years, even though he and his father had made their peace, Burke felt a pang of regret that it had gone so far. But his father's grief over losing Maggie had driven them to the brink of bankruptcy. Adam's actions had sealed the deal.

It was either challenge his father and take over or lose everything that they had worked to achieve.

Burke stroked the memento of that fateful night. Two things had happened then that would forever shape the rest of his life. First, he'd become a man, the leader of his family, the one they would all depend on. And second, he had decided, as he saw his father sobbing in misery over the remnants of what had once been a proud life, that Burke would never let himself need another person the way his father had needed his mother. It was a man's choice, as he saw it. You cannot love one person that much and still have enough left to serve the many who depend on you.

He'd been true to his word on both counts. He'd applied the ruthless business tactics that his father had taught him, slashed jobs, cut the budget to the bone, stripped away bonus plans and reduced salaries, starting with his own. It wasn't enough.

And as for needing anyone?

Need was some other person's weakness. Not his. Ever. Except…

There was his mother's dying wish.

A wish too long ignored.

A job that no one in Mt. Knott could know about, much less help him with.

He *needed* to take care of that.

Christmas was only five weeks away. Time was running out.

He'd looked at his predicament from every possible angle. In order to preserve everything his mother had worked so hard to keep secret for so many years, he would require a certain type of person. Someone from out of town. Someone who would work hard, collect her sizable paycheck and then go away before December twenty-fourth to leave his family and his town to celebrate the sacred holiday, without so much as a backward glance. Someone who shared his beliefs that business is not a personal thing, that sentiment breeds weakness, and that needing someone is not the cornerstone of a good life but a roadblock on the way to the top.

He forced his hat back down low on his head and made his way toward the building at last. He would duck inside and grab the box that had been waiting there for him ever since he had cleared out of his office to make way for Adam. In it he'd find a phone number on a business card. Tomorrow morning, he'd have to make the trek to Atlanta.

Chapter Two

"Working on the day after Thanksgiving, Ms. Hoag? I thought you'd be out shopping with the rest of the country."

"*Shopping?*" It took Dora Hoag a moment to grasp the concept. "Oh, *shopping! Christmas* shopping. As in gifts and glad tidings and ho-ho-ho and 'Hark! the Herald Angels…'"

Dora let out a low sigh.

She glanced up from the paperwork on her enormous desk at the salt-and-pepper–haired man, Zach Bridges, owner of the company who cleaned their office building. She knew him, just as she knew everyone on his cleaning crew, the night security guards, the lunch cart girls, everyone at the nearest all-night coffee shop and the company maintenance staff. Dora knew pretty much anyone who, like her, was still working long after others had gone off to…well, do whatever it was people who did not work *all* the time did when they were *not* working. She knew them, but they didn't know her, not really.

Granted, each year she took off most of the month of December, using up some of the vacation days she hadn't taken during the year. After seven years she thought ol' Zach might have figured out that she did not need more time to go caroling, wrap packages or bake cookies. She was hiding.

Hiding from the hurt the most joyous time of year always had meant to her. After all, what happiness is there in the season of giving when you have no one to give to?

Dora supported all the charities, of course. She'd worked at missions serving food and dropped a mountain of coins in little red buckets. She went to the candlelight service at her church, and her heart filled with love as they sang the hymns about the baby born in the manger. But when the last parishioners had called out their goodbyes, Dora had always been alone. Like the last gift under the tree that nobody claimed.

"Let me guess. You're the type who has all her shopping done before the stores even put up the first display. Oh, say, long about the end of September." Zach's smile stretched beyond the clipped edges of his mustache. "That way you don't have to face the rush this time of year."

Dora would have loved a reason to brave the throng and chaos this time of year to find just the right thing to express how she felt, to make someone smile, to give them…well, just to give from her heart. Instead she had work to do, and if she hoped to take her yearly sabbatical starting next week, she had to get back to it.

She flipped over a piece of paper in the file and narrowed her eyes at the long column of numbers. "I'm shopping all right. I just have a different idea of what constitutes a bargain."

"Looking for a couple of small businesses to snatch up and use as stocking stuffers, eh?"

"Snatch up? You make me sound like a bird of prey swooping down for the kill."

"Eat like a bird," he said, emptying the day's trash—an apple core, a picked-over salad in a plastic container, half a sandwich with just the crusts nibbled away. "And you're always flitting around, never perching anyplace for long."

"I've been based in this office for seven years, now, Zach."

"Seven years, and I'm still dusting the same office chair. Ain't ever in it long enough to wear it out and requisition a new one."

"Point taken." She laughed. For a moment she considered quizzing the man on what else he had concluded about her over the years, but a flashing light and a buzz from her phone system stopped her.

"Ms...." The barely audible voice cut out, followed by another buzz then, "This is..." Silence, another buzz. "...says that..." A longer silence, a buzz, then nothing, not even static.

She frowned.

Zach chuckled and gave a shrug. "Security. Brought in extra help for the holidays and made the new ones work this weekend."

"Not like you, huh, Zach? You let your staff have the time off and came in yourself." She admired that. It showed the character to put others before your own desires and the integrity to make sure you still meet your promised goals.

"Just the way I roll, I reckon," Zach said matter-of-factly. Then he nodded his head toward the bin beneath her paper shredder, his way of asking if she wanted him to take the zillion cross-cut strips of paper away with the rest of the trash.

She shook her head. Nobody got a glimpse of her business, not even in bits and pieces. She glanced down at the pad on her desk and the silly little doodle of a very Zach-like elf pushing a candy-cane broom and suppressed a smile. It was only business, she admitted to herself as she tore off the page and slid it into the middle of the pile of papers waiting for the shredder. The man might come to some conclusions about her on his own, but she wouldn't supply any confirmation. That was the way *she* rolled.

Never show your soft side. Never reveal all your talents, even the more whimsical ones. Never let anyone get a peek at what you think of them. Never share your dreams. Never act on anything in blind trust, not even your own feelings.

And most importantly, never let your hopes or your heart do the work that is the rightful domain of your history and your head.

She'd learned that lesson the hard way and not all that long ago.

She looked at the nest of shredded paper and blinked. Tears blurred her vision. The tip of her nose stung.

For an instant she was in South Carolina on a lovely summer day at a family barbeque. Not *her* family, but one in which she had thought she might one day find a place.

Dora Burdett. How many times had she doodled that name like some young girl in middle school with her first crush? *Crush.* What an apt word for what had happened to that dream.

She cleared her throat, spread her hands wide over the open file before her and anchored herself firmly in the present. "If you'll excuse me, I have to get back to my work."

"Always wheelin' and dealin', huh, Ms. Hoag?"

"I head Acquisitions and Mergers, Zach." She raised her head and stared at the massive logo for GrimExCynergetic Global Com

Limited on the green marble wall beyond her open door, where professional decorators had already begun hanging greenery with Global gold-and-silver ornaments. "It's my job to find the best deals before anyone else does."

"One step ahead of all those poor saps who took the long weekend off to get a jump on the holidays, right?"

"Yeah," she said, her voice barely above a whisper. "Those poor saps."

How she so wanted to be one of them.

All her life that was what she had wanted most of all—to have somebody recognize what she had to give, and to accept it and her. Not as an obligation or duty or in hopes of currying favor but because…she mattered.

Dora had never truly felt that she mattered. She, the things she did, the things she thought, her hopes, her dreams, *her*. Not in that way when someone loves you despite your short-comings. When someone not only wants the best for you but feels you are the best for them, that you bring out the best in each other. She did not grow up in a home like that.

Her mother died when she was born. Her overwhelmed father left his newborn in the

care of a childless and already middle-aged
aunt and uncle while he went away to "find
himself" and "get his head on straight," as
people said in the seventies.

Apparently he never did either thing,
because he never returned for Dora. Sometimes when Dora thought about him she
imagined a man wandering about with his
head facing backward, asking total strangers
if they had seen his lost self.

Aunt Enid and Uncle Taylor did their best
to care for her as their own. They started this
by naming her Dora, which already put her
at a disadvantage among peers with names
like Summer, Montana and Jessica. So she
kept to herself and worked hard, trying to
make her foster parents proud. And for her
effort she drew the attention of teachers and
administrators. They called her "the little
adult" and made jokes about her being "ten
going on forty" and tried to get her to lighten
up a little. But whenever they needed something done—from choosing a child to represent the school at a leadership conference to
helping out in the office or being in charge of
the cash box at the pep club bake sale—they
tapped Dora.

She learned quickly that hard work and efficiency opened doors. It wasn't the same as fitting in or mattering to someone but it came a close second. About as good as Dora thought she'd ever see.

Still, she couldn't help wondering how different her life might be if just once someone had reached out and asked her to come through the doors her drive had created.

A small thing.

A shouted invitation to join a crowded lunch table.

A remembered birthday.

An explanation of why a certain blond-haired, South Carolina gentleman had slammed the door in her face when she had only wanted to…

"I'm dreaming of a…"

"Please, no Christmas songs, Zach."

"Too early in the season for you?" the man asked, as he tossed his dust rag on top of his cart and began to back the cart out of the room.

"Something like that." Especially when her mind had just flashed back to last summer and that family barbeque when she had thought that finally she had done something so caring and constructive that it would change her entire life. That the man she had offered to help, she dared hope, would change her life.

Dora Burdett.

She pressed her eyes closed.

Zach cleared his throat.

A twinge of guilt tightened her shoulders and made her sit upright, look the man in the eyes and produce a conciliatory smile. "Oh, don't get me wrong. I'm not one of those who wants to do away with Merry Christmas or any of the wonderful trappings of the season. I just…"

She put her hand over her forehead, as if that would warm up the old thought process and help her find the right words to explain her feelings. Except, it wasn't her brain that was frozen against all the joyous possibilities Christmas represented to so many. She loved the Lord, and observed His birth in her own way. "I love going to church for the candle-light service on Christmas Eve. I love singing the hymns and all, but…."

"But after that you don't have no one to go home to and share it all with," Zach said softly.

"How did you know that?" The observation left her feeling so exposed she could hardly breathe.

"You don't dust around folks's nicknacks and geegaws or throw out their calendar's pages or run into them working on the day after Thanksgiving year upon year without learning a thing or two about those folks."

The answer humbled her even if it didn't bring her much relief. "I'll bet."

"Anyway, don't think it's my place to say—or sing—anything more, but I hate to leave without at least…" He scratched his head, worked his mouth side to side a couple of times then finally sighed. "I'll just offer this thought."

Dora braced herself, pressing her lips together to keep from blurting out that she didn't need his thoughts or sympathy or songs. Because, deep down, she sort of hoped that whatever he had to say might help.

He lifted his spray bottle of disinfectant cleaner the way someone else might have raised a glass to make a toast. "Here's to hoping this year is different."

It didn't help.

But Dora smiled. At least she thought she

smiled. She felt her face move, but really it could have been anything from a fleeting grin to that wince she tended to make when forcing her feet into narrow-toed high heels. Just as quickly she fixed her attention on the papers in front of her and busied herself with shuffling them about. "Thanks. Now I need to get back to work. Can't make a deal on merely hoping things will improve, can I?"

"On the contrary." The challenge came from the tall blond man who placed himself squarely in her office doorway. "I'd say that hope is at the very core of every deal."

Burke Burdett! Questions blew through Dora's mind more quickly than those fictional eight tiny reindeer pulling a flying sleigh. But the words came out of her mouth fast and furious and from the very rock bottom of her own reality. "How dare you show your face to me."

"Show my face? The view don't get any better from the other side, Dora," he drawled in his low, lazy Carolina accent.

Zach, who had worked the cleaning cart into the hallway by now, laughed.

Dora opened her mouth to remind him it wasn't part of his job description to make assumptions about her or eavesdrop on her and her guests. The squeak, rattle, squeak of the cart told her Zach had already moved on, though. She was alone in her office with Burke Burdett.

But not for long.

She reached out for a button on her phone, hesitated, then raised her eyes to meet those of her visitor.

He had good eyes. Clear and set in a tanned face with just enough lines to make him look thoughtful but still rugged. But if one looked beyond those eyes, those so-called character lines, there was a hard set to his lips and a wariness in his stance.

"Give me one reason not to call security to come up here and escort you out," she said.

"Well, for starters, I don't think the poor kid you've got posted at the front desk knows how to find the intercom button to hear you, much less where your office is." He dropped into the leather wingback directly across from her.

Years ago an old hand had taught Dora that standing was the best way to keep command of an exchange. *Stand. Move. Hold their attention and you hold the reins of the situation.*

Burke had just broken that cardinal rule. And made things worse when he stretched his legs out in front of him, crossed his boots at the ankle to create a picture of ease. He scanned the room, saying, "Besides, he was the one who let me in."

Dora wasn't the only one who noticed and befriended the people everyone else looked right past. "And what did you use to convince that so-green-he's-in-danger-of-being-mistaken-for-a-sprig-of-holly security guard to get him to do that?"

"Use? Me? Why, nothing but the power of my dazzling personality and charm."

"I've been on the receiving end of your charm, Mr. Burdett. It's more drizzle than dazzle." She'd meant it as a joke. A tease, really. Under other circumstances, with another man, maybe even a flirtation.

Burke clearly knew that. All of it. He responded in kind with the softest and deepest of chuckles.

And Dora found herself charmed indeed.

"So the security kid is already sort of on my side in this deal," he summed up.

"Deal?" She stood so quickly that her chair went reeling back into the wall behind her desk. She did not acknowledge the clatter it made. "There is no deal. You made that very clear to me when you cut me out of your family's plans to save the Crumble and get things there back on track."

Last summer, after working his way quickly up the corporate ladder at Global, Adam Burdett had returned to Mt. Knott with a scheme to buy out Carolina Crumble Pattie and get some satisfaction for all the perceived wrongs done against him by his adoptive father. It had all seemed a bit soap operaish to Dora, but as a good businesswoman she knew those were exactly the elements that put other people at a disadvantage in forging a business contract. Emotions. Family. Old hurts. They could push things either way.

In this case, they had eventually gone against Global's proposed buyout. And in favor of Adam Burdett, and by extension, Dora. Together they had the wherewithal to save the company and the desire to do so. It wasn't what either of them had planned, but then love had a way of changing even the most determined minds. Adam's love for Josie—now his wife—his son, his family.

And Dora's for the town of Mt. Knott, its way of life, the thrill of a new venture based on the same kind of Biblical principles that had once motivated Global a few dozen mergers ago. And her love for Burke.

She hadn't loved him right away but by the end of the summer, she thought she did love him. And she thought he loved her back.

Only she hadn't been thinking. She had been feeling and acting on those feelings. Which had brought her full circle, only then she had become the one at a disadvantage in the contract negotiations. Dora was out. Adam was in. Burke had been nowhere to be found.

Burke glanced her way, then went right on surveying their surroundings. "This is a *new* deal that I've come to talk to you about today."

"New deal? Why would I talk to you about a new deal? Or that old deal? You didn't talk to me about that then and I don't want to talk to you about…"

"Look, I'm here now, dazzling or not, with a new deal to discuss. The past is past. I can't change it. Isn't there anything more important for us to talk about than that?"

Only about a million things. Yet given the chance to bring up any of them all Dora could come up with was, "I can't imagine what we'd have to say to one another."

"I can. At least, I have some things I want to say to you."

Her whole insides melted. Not defrosted like an icicle, dripping in rivulets until it had dwindled to nothing but a nub, but more like a piece of milk chocolate where the thumb and finger grasp it—just enough to make a mess of everything.

"You have something to say to me?" She bent her knees to sit, realized her chair was a few feet away and moved around the desk instead to lean back against it. "Like what, for instance?"

"Like…" He tilted his head back. He narrowed his eyes at her. He rested his elbows on the arms of the chair.

The leather crunched softly, putting her in mind of a cowboy shifting into readiness in the saddle. Readiness for what, though?

She held her breath.

He leaned forward as if every decision thereafter depended on her answer, asking softly and with the hint of his smile infusing his words, "Like, what do you want for Christmas?"

She almost slid off the edge of the desk. "I…uh…"

What did she want for Christmas? "After six months of not so much as a phone message, you drove all the way from South Carolina to Atlanta to ask me what I want for Christmas?" She stood up to retake control of what was clearly a conversation with no real purpose or direction. "Are you kidding me? Who does that?"

He could not answer her. Or maybe he could answer but didn't want to. He just sat there.

And sat there.

She could hear him breathing. Slow and steady. See his eyes flicker with some deep emotion but nothing she could define without looking long and hard into them. And she was not likely to do that.

She cleared her throat. She could wait him out. She had waited him out, in fact. He had been the one who had come to her, not the other way around. Even though early on there had been plenty of long, lonely nights when she had wanted nothing more than to hop in her car, or in the company jet or hitch a ride on a passing Carolina Crumble delivery truck to get herself back to South Carolina to confront him. Or kiss him.

Or both.

She wanted to do both. Even now. Which made it imperative that she do something else all together. So she plunked down on the edge of the desk again and said the only thing that made any sense at all to her, given the circumstances. "What I want is for you to go back to Mt. Knott and just leave me in peace."

"Peace. Yes." His slow, steady nod gave the impression of a man who longed for the very same gift—but doubted he'd ever find it. "That I can't promise you. That's better a request for the One who sent his Son."

"Nice save," she whispered, thinking of how deftly he'd avoided her demand for him to leave.

"Best save ever made, if you think about it."

She looked out into the hallway at the Christmas decorations going up. Global would not have a nativity scene, or any reference to the birth of Christ, and yet they covered the place in greenery, the symbol of life everlasting. All around her this time of year, the world came alive with symbols of hope. They rang in the ears, they delighted the eye, they touched the heart. It was such a special time, a time when one could believe not just in the wonder of God's Son but also in the possibilities for all people of goodwill.

Maybe even for a person like Burke.

Maybe he *had* really come here because he wanted to know what she wanted. Maybe he needed to know that she could still want him, to tell her that he had made a mistake, to tell her that she…

He shifted forward again, clasping his hands. "As for me…"

As for me. He had asked what she wanted, ignored her reply and went straight for his real purpose in coming. *Me.*

Himself.

He didn't want to know about her, he wanted to ask her to do something for him.

The moment passed and Dora stood again. She had to get him out of here. She had to keep him from saying another word that might endear him to her, that might give her reason to hope….

"As for you, Mr. Burdett." She moved to the door and made a curt jerk of her thumb to show him the way he should exit. "I don't really care what you want for Christmas."

"Not even if what I want, only you can give me?"

Chapter Three

Burke had broken the first rule of negotiation. He had let his counterpart know the strength of her position. He had been upfront and told her that he wanted to make a deal and she was the only one he wanted to deal with. He might as well have handed her a blank check.

And he would have done just that if he had thought it would work.

It wouldn't. Not with a woman like Dora. So he had done the next best thing, given her all the power in the situation. Now that, that was something she had to find compelling. Right?

Burke swallowed to push down the lump in his throat. He was not accustomed to anyone questioning his judgment and actions. Even when they included his limited charm, fumbling coyness and…Christmas cutesiness.

Who does that? Dora's earlier question echoed in his thoughts. Who drives all the way from South Carolina to Atlanta to ask a grown woman—one who clearly hates his guts—what she wants for Christmas?

Certainly not Top Dawg, the alpha male of the Burdett wolf pack. Certainly not him. And yet, that's exactly what he'd done.

And he had no idea whom to blame for it.

"What do you want, Burke?" She folded her arms over her compact body, narrowed her dark eyes and pursed her lips, a look only Dora could pull off. A look that probably set countless underlings and more than a few superiors shaking in their boots. A look that made Burke want to take her by the shoulders and find the nearest mistletoe. "What could I possibly do for you?"

He forced the obvious and inappropriate answers aside and started at the beginning.

"It's a long story. Goes back to my mom." He squirmed in the fancy wingback. He tried to make himself comfortable but the back was too stiff, the seat too short, the leather too slick. Not to mention that his trying to pin his actions on his late mother, too flimsy.

He wasn't a man who needed to assign blame, it was just that something had brought him to this point and he sure wished he knew what it was.

"Your, um, your *mother?*" Dora did not flinch but her no-nonsense squint did soften as she prodded him to say more.

He jerked his head up and their eyes met. He hadn't planned on that happening. Hadn't prepared for it—hadn't steeled himself against the accusations he saw aimed like a hundred arrows right at him.

How could he have prepared a defense for those? He'd earned each and every one of those unforgiving, poisonous points. She had every right to hate him, or at least not to want to see him and to turn down his proposal outright. "Uh, yeah. My mother. Thing is she started this…it all started a long time ago, really. Long time before she was my mom or met my dad or had any idea that her life would turn out, well, the way it did."

Dora looked away from him at last. Her shoulders sagged, but she kept her chin angled up, in that way she had that she thought made her seem brave and sophisticated.

Seeing her like that made Burke want to push himself up to his feet and take her in his arms and hold her close. To lay his cheek against her soft, black hair and tell her that when she acted that way he could see right through to the scared, lonely little girl he had seen in her since the first time she powered her way into the Crumble to try to buy it out.

She sounded the part, too, quiet with a tiny quiver that she forced to be still more and more with each word. "None of us knows the way our lives will turn out."

"My mom did." He matched her tone, without the tremor. "Or she thought she did."

"That's the kicker, isn't it? When things don't turn out the way you thought they would?" Try as she might to come off all cool and in control, his showing up like this had obviously thrown her off balance. "When you start down a path. You make plans. You pray about it and feel you've finally…"

She glanced out the door.

He uncrossed his ankles and set his feet flat, just in case he decided to up and bolt from the room. It wasn't his style to do that kind of thing, but then again, neither was the way he had treated Dora earlier this year. Something about her made him do things he'd never thought himself capable of.

"Things just don't…" She shuffled the files on her desk.

He looked down. He should have worn his new boots. Dora deserved for him to put his best foot forward, literally and figuratively.

Dora cleared her throat.

He crossed his ankles again, his way of making it harder to give up on his quest and hightail it back to Mt. Knott.

"Like you said," she murmured at last, "…the way you thought."

"Yeah," he said. "That's the kicker. When things don't turn out the way you wished they would."

She'd said *thought*.

He'd said *wished*.

He wondered if she would correct him and in doing so bluntly and unashamedly confirm that they were talking about their own failed plans. If only she would and they could get it out into the open.

Burke was an out-in-the-open kind of man.

Always had been—except when the good faith of a woman who didn't have sense enough to give up on him was at stake. That's how he'd gotten into this predicament in the first place.

He'd wanted to be upfront with Dora from the get-go, but the underhanded way in which his brothers had cut him from his spot as top dog of the family business left him hurt, humiliated and wanting to tuck his tail between his legs and hide. He knew that about himself. Knew that what he'd done, dumping her by pretending the only thing between them had been a business deal, was wrong. If she would only call him on it maybe they could sort it out and then…then *what?*

He shook his head. "You see, my mom, she had this plan for her life."

Dora held her tongue.

He felt he had to forge ahead.

Fill the silence.

State his case for coming here after all this time.

And if he got what was coming to him in the bargain? He'd take it like he took every blow and disappointment he'd suffered in life, without flinching and letting anyone see his pain.

"College, travel, adventure. Mom had the brains, the courage and the means to do it all. Something I know you can relate…" Too soon. One look into her eyes and he could see he had tried to get her to invest in this on a personal level much too soon.

"Yes?"

No, not too soon. He'd read her all wrong.

He'd spent hour upon hour with her. They'd discussed everything from business to barbeque sauce. He'd even sat by her side and mapped out a future that would forever intertwine them, if only on their corporate income tax papers.

The things unsaid had promised more, and he knew it. Their laughter, their shared beliefs, their dedication to their work. Those things made it easy to be around Dora, something he'd never felt with another woman. They also made it easy to let go of her when their business deal fell through.

Fell through. Pretty words for having been kicked out by your own family and finding yourself left with nothing more to offer anyone, least of all a woman like Dora.

No position. No power. No purpose.

Burke knew that Dora needed those things for herself and from anyone involved with her. After the family had put those—position, power, purpose—out of reach for him, a personal relationship with Dora had become impossible for him.

He pressed on with his pitch. "My mother changed her life plans completely so that she could give her all to her family and the new dreams we would create together."

Dora would never have done the same.

"So your mother made her choice," she said. "Most women do. We tell ourselves we can have it all, and maybe we can but most of us know we can't have it all and give our all, all the time. So we all make choices. That *is* something I can relate to."

There was an eagerness in Dora's eyes, an intensity. Did he dare call it hope? Or merely an openness to hope? It was so slim, so faint. He doubted she even knew she was revealing it. It embarrassed him a little and humbled him that he should have this advantage, no, this blessing. That he should get this tiny glimpse into something so personal, the best part of this woman he admired so much.

Not until this moment did he realize that while Dora Hoag might be living the life his mother had never realized, it was not by her own choosing.

That changed everything—save for the fact that he still couldn't pull off any of this without someone's help. Dora's help. But now instead of wheeling and dealing to get it, he knew he had to win her over, make her want to do it as much as he wanted her to do it.

Without giving her any warning, he stood and held his open hand toward her. "Let's get out of here."

She looked at his outstretched palm then at the door. "You go first."

"Stop playing games, Dora."

"At the risk of sounding repetitive—you first."

"I don't play games." He dropped his hand.

"I know." She folded her arms again. "And you don't make a trip to tell someone something face-to-face that could easily be said on the phone or by e-mail."

He acknowledged that with a dip of his head.

"So just say what you came here to say and then kindly get out," she said quite unkindly.

"You're right. I did come to tell you something. And ask you something. But first I have to show you." He reached into his inside coat pocket.

Her arms loosened slightly. Her shoulders lifted. "If you were any other man, I'd expect you to pull out a small velvet box after a statement like that."

"Small? Velvet?" His fingers curled shut inside his coat. "Oh!"

She tilted her head and gave him a smile that was light but a bit sad. "I don't play games, either."

"I'll say you don't." He shook his head. She'd gotten him. He'd come here thinking he knew what he was walking into and how to maintain control of it and she'd gotten him. To his surprise, he didn't mind. In fact, he kind of liked it. He liked this feisty side of her. "But you sure do a have an overactive imagination, lady."

"Overactive? Because I once thought of you as a man of his word?"

Suddenly he liked that feistiness a little less. "Hey, let's not go there, Dora."

"Where else would you like to go, Burke? You seem to be up for a lot of travel all of a sudden. Coming here. Wanting me to go someplace with you. Maybe we should add a little trip down memory lane to your itinerary."

"Memory lane?" He smirked.

"What?" Lines formed in her usually smooth forehead. She pursed her lips and waited for him to say more.

"Just a pretty old-fashioned term, don't you think? I'd have gone for a play on time travel." He was trying to lighten the mood.

She wasn't having any part of it. "I was raised in a pretty old-fashioned home by my great-aunt and uncle. It's the way they talked, I guess. It's not so unusual. You knew the meaning."

The meaning he knew. The tidbit about her upbringing he hadn't known. Did it make any difference? Probably not to his plan, but it did explain a few things about her outlook on the world and the world's outlook on her. Nobody got her, not really. Nobody knew her.

Try as he could to stop it, Burke found that she was bringing out the protective nature of his Top Dawg personality again. To keep from caving into that or allowing her to rehash how badly he had handled things between them last summer, he stepped forward. He pulled the business card he had gone to retrieve from the Crumble out of his pocket. He gazed at the off-white rectangle with raised black lettering atop brightly colored shapes for only a moment before he handed it to her.

"What's that?"

"That's where I want to take you."

"To a doctor's office?"

"A pediatrician's office."

"Why?"

He moved to the doorway. "Come with me and I'll explain everything."

She did not budge. "So far, you haven't explained anything. You haven't answered a single one of my questions. Why should I let you show me this place?"

"Showing is simple." He held out his hand again. "Answers are complicated."

She ignored his gesture and raised one arched, dark eyebrow. "Then uncomplicate them."

Uncomplicate a lifetime of mischief, hope, happiness, tough choices and intricate clandestine arrangements? Couldn't be done.

Rattle. Squeak. Rattle.

Zach and his cleaning cart went wobbling by the open door.

Burke grinned. Maybe he couldn't just hand her the whys and wherefores of his situation, but if Dora wanted answers he could at least give her one. "You asked me who comes all the way from South Carolina to Atlanta to ask someone what they want for Christmas. It's not so hard to figure out, really, if you think about it."

Zach's raspy voice rang out in a Christmas carol about Santa Claus.

Dora frowned.

Burke jerked his head toward the open door. "Go ahead. Say it. You know you want to. Who makes a trip to ask someone what they want for Christmas?"

"S-Santa Claus?" she whispered, as Zach rounded the corner and his song faded.

Burke gave a small nod of his head, then looked up to catch her eye and winked. "That's me. And if there is going to be Christmas in Mt. Knott this year, I am going to need your help."

Chapter Four

"Okay, we've been driving for fifteen minutes." Dora glanced out the window of his shiny silver truck. Her, tooling around Atlanta in a pick up with a South Carolina snack cake cowboy Santa-wannabe at the wheel—listening to country music's finest, crooning Christmas carols on the radio. What happened to her policy of not trusting anyone, especially anyone named Burdett, again? What happened to her plan of ditching Christmas again this year by making herself scarce before sundown? What happened to this place that Burke had promised to show her, the one that would give her a reason to forgo the not trusting and the ditching and make her want to…

The lyrics to a song she'd heard moments before—"I Saw Mommy Kissing Santa Claus"—popped into her head. Burke Burdett? *Santa?* Difficult to imagine. Kissing him? Hardly the kind of thing a serious businesswoman, an angry almost-girlfriend or a woman of good Christian character ought to be dwelling on! She stole a peek at his rugged profile and noted the way he seemed to fill up the cab of the truck and yet still leave a place for her to sit comfortably beside him.

"Burke?"

"Hmm?" He didn't look at her and yet the casualness of his reply gave her a sense of familiarity no quick cast-off glance in a truck cab ever could.

She flexed her fingers on the padded car door handle and forced herself to study their surroundings as she counted off their recent itinerary. "I've seen the art gallery where some lady from Mt. Knott had her first show. The jeweler's where your mother used to have special ornaments engraved. And the building of the accounting firm that employs the valedictorian of your graduating class."

She hoped she hadn't missed anything.

He'd told her it would all make sense in time so, ever the bright, obedient girl, she had tried to make mental notes as they drove along.

"Yeah?" He seemed engrossed in reading the street signs.

If he didn't know where they were going then why had he brought her along? And why had she come? She squeezed her eyes shut to put her thoughts back on track.

She crossed her arms and tipped up her chin. "So far you haven't really shown me anything that supports your claim of needing me to help you play the jolly fat guy."

"Hey." He tapped the brake lightly and stole a sly, amused glimpse her way at last. "Is that any way to talk to Santa?"

"*You* are not Santa."

"Maybe not," he conceded, with an expression that was neither jeering nor jovial but somewhere in between. Then he made a sharp turn, and used the momentum of their shifting center of gravity to lean over and whisper, just beside her ear, "But I'm on his team."

"Oh, right." She shivered at his nearness. "Team Santa. I suppose you have the T-shirt and matching ball cap?"

"No can do. Team Santa is strictly a hush-hush kind of deal." He sat upright behind the wheel again and fixed his eyes straight ahead. "Not that I would look devastatingly cute in said hat and shirt."

He would. He'd be downright adorable, with his suntanned skin and deep set eyes that twinkled when he knew he had the best of a person in a given situation—and Burke always had the best of everyone in any situation. He knew it and so did she.

She couldn't take her eyes off him now. So strong, so confident, so manly but with just a hint of boyish excitement over this odd adventure he insisted on dragging her into. This was the Burke she had known last summer. The one she had wanted so much to give her heart to, right up until his last quick, cutting phone call when he'd ended their professional and, by extension, personal relationship based on the results of the family meeting. Correction: the Carolina Crumble Pattie board of directors meeting, a board made up of the members of the Burdett family. This Burke and the man who had torn her dreams to shreds with a soft-spoken and deceptively simple, "nothing personal, just business," seemed to be two entirely different people.

A man like that…he was not to be trusted.

That reminder made it easier for her to sit back and create a little verbal distance. "I suppose next you will try to tell me that you're an elf?"

"Why do you think I let my hair get this shaggy?" He tapped the side of his head. "To hide my pointed little ears."

"Really?" She did not look his way. "I thought you let your hair grow out for the same reason I keep mine short."

"Because it makes you look like a little girl all dressed up in grown-up clothes?"

"No." She crinkled up her nose at his way-off-base guess. "Because…um, does it?"

She put her hand to the back of her head. If anyone else on earth had said that she'd have given them what for, but coming from Burke, it had a sweetness that took her by surprise. She had always suspected that he could see the young Dora, the frightened, lonely and longing-to-belong child who lurked just beneath her polished surface. The notion warmed her heart. And chilled her to the core.

"That's not…that is…the point is, we

both keep our hair the length we do for the same reason."

"I hope not. My hair is long but I hope not long enough to make me look like a little girl!"

"I like your hair." It wasn't all that long, really, just grown out enough to add to the overall appeal of this man who was rough-hewn, unfettered by convention and free from any kind of vanity or fussiness.

"Do you?" he asked softly.

"Yeah," she said, more softly. Almost childlike, almost flirty. The CD had stopped playing a few minutes earlier and she didn't have to compete with sleigh bells and steel guitars to be heard.

He looked into her eyes for only a moment before he squared his broad shoulders and stuck out his chest. "Then I guess I'll cancel my regular appointment with the barber."

"You don't keep any regular appointments with a barber, Burke. Just like I never *miss* mine." She sat in the truck with posture so perfect that only the small of her back made contact with the upholstery. "I wear my hair short for the same reason you don't bother to keep yours trimmed. I'm too busy with my work to bother with upkeep and style."

He did not dispute that, just turned the wheel and took them down a quiet residential street in a part of town Dora had never seen before.

They fell silent.

The air went still around them.

Dora should have let it go. Let him make the next move, the next comment. He had brought her here to prove something, after all. She didn't need to ramble on, cajoling and teasing and then retreating, hoping he would follow. That phase between them had passed. Now it really was just business.

Nothing personal. Just business.

No, not even business.

Once he had shown her the last of these places—he seemed to think they would add up to something that would somehow affect her—and shared this story of his, she'd probably never see him again. If she were smart she'd just keep her mouth zipped and wait it out until he dropped her off back at her office building.

"So if your hair hides your ears then I guess you wear that cowboy hat of yours all the time to hide your pointed little head?" So much for keeping her mouth shut.

"Elves don't have pointed heads." He frowned. Actually *frowned* as if he had to think that over and make the point quite clear.

She gulped in a breath so she could launch into an explanation that she had meant it as a joke.

He beat her to it by adding, with a wink, "It's just our pointy little hats make it look that way."

She laughed at the very idea of Burke in a pointed hat. "Someone sure is aiming to get on the naughty list."

"Aww, you haven't been that bad. Lots of people make cracks about elves and helpers and Santa's weight issues."

"I wasn't talking about me. I was talking about you, for fibbing about wearing a pointed hat."

"I'm not fibbing." He looked quite serious, but couldn't hold it and broke into a big grin. "And I have the photo to prove it."

"Then prove it."

"Uh, I, uh, I don't have the photo with me."

She shook her head. "For a second there, you almost had me believing you."

He went quiet then. Not silent, not still, but

quiet with all the power, control and even reverence that implied. She could hear the tires on the road, the squeak of the seat cushions, the beating of their two battered hearts.

Her skin tingled. Her throat went dry.

For only a moment it was like that, then Burke turned to her, his intense, serious eyes framed by playful laugh lines as he whispered, "Believe me, Dora."

Oh, how she wanted to—to believe him about the hat, his being Santa and, most of all, that he needed her in a way that he needed no one else in the world.

But life had taught her that those kinds of beliefs only led to disappointment. So she kept it light, played along. "You in an elf hat?"

His eyes twinkled. "With red and green stripes, a plump pom-pom and a brass jingle bell on the end."

"What are you going to tell me next?"

"That this is what I wanted you to see." He pulled into a parking lot, slid the truck into a space and cut the engine. "This is why I need you."

"To go to a pediatrician? What? You need me to hold your hand while the doctor holds your tongue down with a Popsicle stick and makes you say 'ahh'?" What was he trying to pull?

"No. Not to go to the doctor, to see what she's doing."

"What? Seeing patients?"

"On the Friday after Thanksgiving." He nodded, his gaze scanning the lot.

Dora took a moment to follow his line of vision. It did not take long for her to come to a conclusion. "This is some kind of clinic?"

"Every Friday, even holidays—except Christmas and when the Fourth of July falls on Friday." He watched as a little boy scurried ahead of a young woman carrying a baby and then held the door to the office open. "A clinic for people who have jobs but no insurance. Just the doc's way of giving back because once upon a time somebody did something nice for her."

"And what does that have to do with Santa Claus coming to Mt. Knott, South Carolina?"

He hesitated a moment, gripping then repositioning his large, lean hands on the steering wheel. He started to speak, held back, then took a deep breath. Finally, he worked his broad shoulders around so that they pressed against the window and his upper body faced her. His brow furrowed. His eyes fixed on her then shifted toward the children. He kept his voice low as if he thought one of them might hear. "Do you know the story of the first Santa, the real Saint Nicholas?"

She kept her backbone pressed to the seat and her cool gaze on the man. "I think the real question here is, do you know how to answer a question directly when it's put to you?"

"Humor me," he said with grim sobriety just before he broke into a crooked grin.

It was the grin that got her. She sighed. "The real Saint Nicholas? Hmm. Turkish? Skinny fellow, too, not the bowlful of jelly Clement Moore described. Or the ho-ho-hokey, soda pop–swilling, round-cheeked invention of American advertising."

"Right. The Bishop of Turkey. He surreptitiously gave bags of gold to girls who otherwise would not have had a dowry so they wouldn't be pressed into servitude or prostitution."

Now she moved around in the seat, impressed. Suspicious but definitely impressed. "You said that like a kid reading off a plaque in a museum."

"Close. Only the museum is my mom's office in the attic of our family home, and the plaque is a caption under an old print from a book she has framed there."

"Really?"

"Really."

"I'd like…"…*to see it someday.* The rest of the sentence went unfinished. She had no business inviting herself, not only into the home where Burke had grown up, but into his late mother's office. "I'd like to know how that relates to this pediatrician's office in Atlanta?"

"Easy. The original saint gave money to girls in order to give them the power to make better lives for themselves, and by extension better lives for their families and their communities."

"And this doctor is doing the same?"

"Because?"

"Because she…" Dora looked at the office once again. On the sign with the doctor's name was the symbol of a gold coin with a wreath encircling a Christmas stocking. "Because once upon a time that doctor got a visit from Saint Nick?"

"Who is?"

"You."

"My mom." His gaze dropped for a moment and the grief seemed so real and still so fresh in him that Dora did not know how to respond. She didn't have the chance, as he quickly recovered and met her gaze with his sad and solemn eyes. "From the time she decided to stay in Mt. Knott and raise a family instead of traveling the world, my mother gave out grants and scholarships to deserving girls and young women who otherwise would not have had the opportunity to make better lives for themselves."

"Wow. She paid for their college?"

"She helped. And not just college. Private high schools. Vocational training. Trips. Conferences. Art supplies."

"Art…oh, art supplies. So the artist, the jeweler, the accountant were all…"

"Just the artist and accountant. The jeweler is where she has the gold medallions engraved that she gave the recipients to let them know they were chosen."

"She didn't present them in some kind of ceremony?"

"She kept it quiet. The jeweler sent them from here so no one would ever know who they came from."

"People suspected the Burdetts, though. They'd have to."

"If they did, no one ever said."

Dora studied the coin with new eyes and understanding. "There's writing around the edge."

"'We give to others because God first gave Christ to us,'" he said, without even looking at the sign or the coin he had just quoted.

"And no one knows about your mother's good works? Really?"

"Only the accountant who manages the financial side of things, me and now you."

"Not even your brothers? Or your dad?"

"It's a secret Mom entrusted with me alone on her deathbed."

"Oh, Burke." She reached out to touch his face, to lend support and comfort.

"But me alone? I don't think I'm up for the job."

Job. Only business. She curled her fingers closed and put her fist to her chest.

"That's why I need your help. I need someone who isn't from Mt. Knott to help me pull this off. Because as a Burdett I can't do anything in Mt. Knott in secret."

"Including taking me out there to manage

this for you," she reminded him, switching swiftly into organizational problem-solving mode. "How would you ever explain that?"

"Oh. Yeah." He scowled. "Unless…"

"Yes?" She needed him to come up with this solution, not because she didn't have one to offer, but because it was his project. She had no intention of investing in it emotionally or even mentally unless he could find a way to win her over to it. Which meant she wasn't getting involved.

"Well, you were out there all last summer and no one questioned that."

"I was in negotiations to buy into your business then." She folded her arms and clamped them down tight. "I don't suppose you want to revisit that?"

"There's a lot about last summer I'd like to revisit."

And a lot of memories she wanted to send packing. She shut her eyes. "Burke, I…"

"Just come out and stay at the family compound, Dora."

"What?"

"We won't have to say why you're there. People probably wouldn't believe anything we told them anyway."

"I can't just leave work." It was the first thing that came to her mind. Not a lie or a means of deceiving him but just a gut reaction, telling the man the kind of thing he'd expect her to say.

The crooked grin returned. He shook his head slowly. "You save up all your vacation time all year and take it in December."

"How did you know that? Did Zach tell you?"

"Who?"

"Zach, the…" The closet thing she had to an old friend. She sighed. "Never mind. Just tell me how you knew that."

"Because you told me."

"I did?"

"One night when we talked about the future. You said if you ever got married you'd want it to be in December."

Her cheeks grew hot. She found it hard to swallow. Marriage? The future? She remembered that night, but not the things they had said—just the way it felt to be near Burke, to sit out on the porch beneath a blanket of stars. Had she really let her guard down so completely? "Was I under the influence of Carolina Crumble Patties?"

"Maybe."

"Sugary foods get to me, you know. Make me say things I don't necessarily mean." As did certain men.

"You meant this."

"You said a lot of things I thought you meant, Burke."

He did not say a word in his own defense.

He couldn't, she realized. And just that quickly she also understood that she could not help him, even with this worthy cause. She could not allow herself to be that vulnerable again, especially not at Christmas.

She looked out at the doctor's office building again. "Just because I don't go into my office most of December doesn't mean I don't have things to do."

"Yeah. Right." He nodded, his eyes downcast. "Everybody has things to do. We live in a busy, busy world. So busy doing the things we have to do we often let go of the things we should do."

That stung. It was true of course, which was probably *why* it stung. "Burke, I—"

"Oh, I don't mean you specifically, Dora." He looked at her, then at the pediatrician's sign, his face stormy with emotion. "Over the years my mom has given out a lot of time and money, and none of those people have ever tried to find out who their benefactor was so they could offer support."

"But this is good," she held her hand out to indicate the clinic taking place right before their eyes.

"Yeah, this is good, but I can't help thinking."

"What?"

"We have kids in Mt. Knott, too."

"What?"

"Everyone always says, why doesn't the Crumble factory do more? Why don't the Burdetts help out the town more? But how many of them ask, what more can I do?"

"I'm not from Mt. Knott," she felt compelled to remind him. She did not owe the town or its inhabitants anything. But then, who was she indebted to? Beyond her aunt and uncle and the unseen powers-that-be at Global? No one. No one needed her on a personal level.

"People don't seem to see that every doctor who goes someplace else to practice, every young person who goes off to college and never comes home, every citizen who gets his gas, does the grocery shopping or sets up business outside of Mt. Knott takes something vital away from the community. The Crumble and the Burdetts can't counteract all that."

"I know."

"We shouldn't have to try."

"I know."

"I just keep thinking that at some point somebody is going to step up."

"That's why you keep the Santa gifts a secret, isn't it?"

"Huh?"

"You're a big softie, admit it."

"Well, thank you for that much."

"But you could put some stipulations on the gifts. Say the recipients have to give something back to Mt. Knott, serve the town a certain amount of time."

"I couldn't do that. Mom never did and I want to carry on her tradition."

"Tradition shcmadition. You do it because you have faith."

"I'm a man of faith, yes, but—"

"Faith in your fellow man. And woman, for that matter."

"I don't know what you mean."

"'We give to others because God first gave Christ to us.'" She read the words from the coin on the sign. "You want to keep this all a big secret because you are hoping that one day one of these girls who are gifted will turn around and do the right thing and give back to the town because they want to, not because they have to."

He didn't deny it but he didn't jump on her claim and praise her for seeing right into his thought process, either.

"Or, at the very least, that the town's people, knowing somebody among them has done these good things, will want to do something for the town, too."

"Is that a crazy thing to hope for?"

"That you hope to inspire people and make it easier for them to give to others?" It was all she had ever wanted. And the very thing she had worked so hard to keep herself from doing. Until now. "No, I think it's wonderful, especially at Christmastime."

"I can't do it alone."

"You don't have to, Burke."

"You mean?"

"I hope you saved that hat you said you had." She could not believe she was saying this but…well, she had known he would have to sell her on the idea to get her to join in. She also knew that the best sales were made by a person who truly believed in what he was selling. Burke, in his own raggedy, begrudging way, believed in Christmas and in his mother's dream. It was within Dora's power to help him realize that dream—a gift only she could give him. How could she refuse? "I may have to borrow it if I plan on becoming this year's Santa's helper."

Chapter Five

Monday was soon enough to get started. Too soon, really, for Burke's tastes. Yet, by his mother's standards, they were already eleven months behind schedule. For her, the undertaking she called the Forgotten Stocking Project was not a special holiday event but a year-round commitment.

If he had let Dora have her way they would have gone to work the day she accepted the position as his assistant. Why not? It's not like she had a bunch of family hovering around for the weekend wondering why she wasn't there diving into the leftovers with the rest of them. Or asking a lot of questions that they considered to show concern but really hinted that she needed to be doing something different with her life.

So, when will you be bringing someone special home for the holidays?

Don't you get lonely in that big house all by yourself?

Now that you aren't working at the Crumble practically twenty-four/seven why don't you start something new? Like, say a family of your own?

He didn't know whether to pity Dora or envy her for not having to endure that. He looked around at the people gathered in Josie's Home Cookin' Kitchen, at the people he had known most of his life chatting with friends and loved ones, then at his sister in-law, *the* Josie of the Home Cookin' in the restaurant's name, and decided, in his grudging curmudgeonly way, that he did not envy Dora. Pity might have gone too far, but he did wish that Dora didn't seem so very alone in this world.

She'd mentioned her father. Gone off to find himself when she was still quite young. He wondered why with all her resources she hadn't tried to locate him.

She had probably weighed the risks

against the potential gains and had come to the most practical conclusion. Dora was first and foremost a businesswoman, after all. Right?

Of all the people who knew Dora Hoag, Burke suspected he above all knew better than that. Dora was so much more than a businesswoman. She was the child she had been and the friend she could be, a good listener, smart, funny, a thoughtful Christian and a…a woman.

Dora was a woman, with all the faults and every fine quality that came with being one. But she had no person to share her joy with and no trusted friend to lean on when things did not go well.

Except she did. She had both, in him. Only maybe she didn't see it that way.

Burke settled onto a stool at the counter. He pulled out a menu, even though he'd had breakfast a few hours earlier and it wasn't quite time for lunch. He'd arrived only a few minutes before the hour he and Dora had agreed to meet. He'd planned that so he wouldn't have time for a lot of chitchat with the patrons, but it also meant he wouldn't have time for a piece of pie. If Dora would be anything—and to his way of thinking, Dora Hoag could be many, many things—she would be prompt.

"Coffee?" Josie lifted up a sturdy white cup turned upside down on a matching saucer.

Burke watched her, thinking how blessed his brother Adam was to have found someone like Josie.

"Sure." He nodded then slid the menu back in place, glad not to have to order something as a cover for hanging around the place. "Surprised to see you here today."

"Why?" Josie paused, his coffee cup still in her hand, to take money from a customer.

Ching. The cash register rang out. Its drawer popped open.

Josie tucked the exact change away then thanked the customer with a radiant smile and a soft word.

Burke squinted as he tried to figure her out. "Thought you'd given up all this to be a full-time mom."

"A *what?*"

"A, uh, a full-time mom?" Burke usually didn't have that much trouble making himself heard or understood.

"That's what I thought you said." *Whomp.*

She sent the cash drawer slamming shut with a swing of her hip.

"Uh-oh," Warren, one of two older fellows who occupied the stools at the diner almost every morning of the week, ducked his head.

Burke sat perfectly still, unsure what was headed his way.

"Burke Burdett!" Josie set the cup down firmly enough to make it clatter against the saucer. "Every mother is a full-time mother!"

With a flare of authority that made it clear she thought she had given the final answer on that, Josie spun around and nabbed the coffeepot.

He frowned. He should have let it go. He'd said what he'd said, she'd said what she said and…and she'd gotten the last word. Being Top Dawg, he just couldn't drop that bone. "I thought some of them were working mothers."

"What?" Josie held the coffeepot back as if she had half a mind not to serve him at all after that remark.

"Oooh. Should have just said 'yes ma'am' and quit while you was ahead," muttered Jed, Warren's cohort in café commentary. "You ain't getting no pie, after a remark like that, no sir."

"Yup. That boy's definitely going on the no-pie list," Warren confirmed, his head shaking forlornly.

"I mean, uh, *every* mother is a working mother?" Burke tried to slip back into his sister-in-law's favor by saying what he thought she wanted to hear. What did he know about this motherhood business, anyway? He'd always sort of thought that he'd raised himself, looked after himself. He hadn't really needed his mom for much. What was the big deal?

"That's better." Josie exhaled and took a second to regain her composure.

"Whew." Burke pretended to wipe his brow for the benefit of Jed and Warren, his counter-mates.

They chuckled.

"And I'm down here today because the place still has my name on it and I intend to keep a hand in running it. Also, I had to come to oversee the end-of-the-month paperwork." Josie approached the counter again. "Your turn."

"Huh?" Burke dragged the saucer and cup closer in front of him on the counter and flipped the cup over.

"I could say the same about being surprised to see you here." Josie held the pot up. The dark brew sloshed, sending its warm, rich aroma wafting his way. "The way you took off the day after Thanksgiving we all half-expected not to see or hear from you again until we got a postcard from you halfway around the world."

"Saying I'd joined some far-off army rather than spend the coming holidays with y'all?" He chuckled, though now that he thought of it maybe that wasn't a bad alternative, once this whole Santa mess got worked out.

"That's what the guys thought. The girls…" She dipped her head and the curls of her ponytail fell over her shoulder as if every part of her had to move in close to get in on this tidbit. "The girls thought maybe it would say you'd run off and eloped and were on an extended honeymoon."

He jerked his head up to meet her gaze. "Married? I don't even have a girlfriend."

"You don't have to have a girlfriend to get married, Burke." Josie laughed. "No one ever thought of me as Adam's girlfriend. I was his baby's adoptive mother, then I was a thorn in his paw, the next thing anyone knew, I was his wife."

Wife? Burke winced. Had he given anyone reason to think that he and…the one woman on the planet he had allowed to become the thorn in his paw…had ever considered…

"Who is getting married?" Warren wanted to know.

"Why do you care, you old coot? Ain't like they plan to invite you along on that fancy honeymoon." Jed gave his companion a nudge in the shoulder. "Way I hear it your wife wasn't too keen on you tagging along on your own honeymoon."

Jed laughed.

Warren joined in, grumbling something that sounded partly like a complaint about his friend's sense of humor and just a little bit like agreement with his assessment.

Burke tensed. He'd spent so much time with his head buried in the business of late that he had forgotten how easily gossip got started in this town.

Gossip? About his super-secret project involving his mother's dying wish and his… his…Dora?

Josie had already gone all demure and

amused, looking down as if the task of pouring coffee, something she did a hundred times a day, required her utmost attention. She lifted the pot.

"On second thought…" Burke stuck his hand over the cup.

Too late.

Josie pulled up but not before a stream of steaming hot liquid splashed over his knuckles.

"I'm so sorry." Josie winced.

He yanked his hand away and, knowing every eye and, more importantly, ear in the place had suddenly fixed on him, gritted his teeth and merely said, "My fault."

He slid from the stool and wiped his hand on a paper napkin from the dispenser on the counter.

"Come back into the kitchen and run that under some cool water." She motioned toward the open door a few steps behind her.

"No, I'm not staying." He wadded the napkin up and, realizing the large trash bin was across the room, stuffed it into his pocket rather than prolong his time there. "I can't stay."

What a bad idea to meet Dora here. He had to get out before she came strolling through that door and fueled who knew how many rumors, spreading from this point like wheel spokes in every direction, to every home and family and inquiring mind in Mt. Knott. Ex-business partner, thorn in his paw, soon to be wife. The town would have them married before they finished their Christmas shopping!

He checked his watch. She was already a few minutes late. Not like Dora. He didn't have any time to…

"Sorry, I'm late." Dora stood in the open front door with a space-aged looking gizmo attached to one ear, her hair an uncharacter-istic mess. Fresh but still formidable. Without her power pumps to give her height or her tailored business suit to give her substance, she looked like a cross between a waif arriving at the gates of an infamous orphan-age and one of those bright-eyed girls with big dreams getting off the bus in the big city. She wore a black fuzzy sweater, a single strand of pearls, some black-and-white checked pants and black shoes. With bows.

It was the bows that got to Burke. He didn't think he'd ever before seen her wear anything so out of character and yet so perfect.

She clutched her expensive leather briefcase to her chest, blinked those big, brown eyes and blew away a piece of straw that had tangled in the soft curl of black hair alongside her cheek. "I'd blame traffic but, well, is getting behind a slow-moving tractor hauling hay considered traffic around here?"

"Dora?" Josie, still standing close to the kitchen door, cocked her head. *"Dora Hoag?* Talk about being surprised to see somebody in here!"

A murmur moved through the room.

It had the effect of a bucket of cold water on Burke's head—a most unpleasant wake-up call but one that got the job done and quick.

Think fast, Burke warned himself. No. Act fast. That's what this situation called for. To act fast, talk fast and think about what he had done later.

"Yeah! What a surprise to see you come walking through that door today at, uh…" Another glance at his watch. "…Ten minutes after ten in the morning."

"What? Did we get our wires crossed? Is this the wrong day? Wrong place? Wrong… what's wrong, Burke?" Dora spoke softly as though he were the only person in the room.

He liked that feeling.

Liked it a lot.

Too much.

He cleared his throat and took her by the upper arm, turning to, in essence, present her to the room and to emphasize to her that they were not alone. Then he leaned down and whispered for her ears only, "Play along, please."

"Play? Burke, what's going on?" she managed to ask, barely moving her lips.

Cool trick but not one a bulldog of a man like him, accustomed to barking out orders meant to be heard and carried out, could pull off. So he faked a cough and used his fist to hide his mouth as he said, "For the sake of secrecy. We can't be seen planning in a public place like this."

"No lies," she commanded, under the cover of slapping him on the back in a show of helping him with his sudden coughing fit.

Slapped him a bit harder than the pretense called for, he thought, but then maybe she felt she deserved the indulgence for the way his family had treated her. The way he had treated her. The way he was treating her right now.

"Okay, no lies." Even though lying would have been the easiest way to go. But it was Christmas and he was supposed to be a better man this time of year, right? "Not that I make lying a way of life, you know."

She shot him a look that suggested she did not know that.

It hurt but he understood her position.

"So, what are you doing in town?" Josie had made her way around the counter now and had her hand out to Dora, the woman who had been her husband's boss at Global not so long ago.

"Me? I, um, I have some time off," Dora blurted out.

"So you invited her here for the holidays?" Josie took Dora's hand but her eyes focused on Burke.

"No!" That was the truth. He fully expected Dora to be gone before the holidays rolled around. Once she'd finished her part in the vetting and selection process, he expected her to hightail it out of town to leave him, the town and his nosy, matchmaking family to tolerate, um, *celebrate* Christmas as usual.

He glanced down at Dora.

Usual? How could he carry on as usual knowing she was alone in the world during the season when so many, like it or not, came together with their loved ones?

"That is, I didn't invite her to spend the holidays with us but—"

"He told me about Mt. Knott this time of year and I wanted to come and see it for myself." Dora released Josie's hand then looked up into Burke's eyes, her expression reassuring him that she would not insinuate herself on him or his family. "I came of my own volition. I'll only stay as long as I feel welcome."

Burke felt like a jerk. Probably because he was one, from the way he had roped her into helping him, to the way he was treating her this moment. Then and there he vowed he would do something to make it up to her. Somehow. Someday.

"Well, as far as I'm concerned you are welcome to stay the whole season." Josie beamed. "Ring in the New Year with us, if you like."

"The New Year?" Burke scowled. Jerk or not he had no intention of having Dora Hoag all but move into this town—this very small, very up-in-everybody's-business town.

"Oh, I plan to be back at work the day after Christmas. I always am," she said, before Burke had the chance to say something awful that would hurt or embarrass her. "Like I said, I just came for, well, because Burke had said…it just seemed right to, well, you know. You all know your little town better than I do, surely you understand why I came."

Get the other guy to tell you his strengths and in doing so, you will discover where you need to be stronger. Burke recognized that Dora had the finely honed people-assessing skills of a seasoned CEO or sales executive. If the folks around them asserted that she had surely come here for the fresh air, she'd need to make sure they saw her soaking up plenty of it. If they discerned she must be trying to buy out the Burdetts again, then by simply spending time around the Crumble every day she would fuel that rumor and throw everyone off the scent of her real objective. And if anyone guessed the real reason? Ha! Who in this town would guess she had come to Mt. Knott to play Santa's helper?

It was an old negotiating technique that

Dora had, after a few false starts, fallen back on. She was clever, he'd give her that. And sharp witted. And—

He gazed down at her, smiling right at the two men sitting at the counter even as her knuckles went white on the handle of her briefcase.

And adorable. Dora was adorable.

"So?" she prodded. "Y'all know why I'm here, right?"

Another murmur went through the room. Josie frowned.

A woman in a booth started to say something then thought better of it and shook her head.

Finally Warren sputtered in disgust, "Oh, c'mon, y'all," and slapped his leg. "Ain't it obvious? She come to participate in our fabulous downtown hoedown, all around, by the pound, glory bound…. Stop me, Jed, I can't seem to get to the end of this thing!"

"You got the name wrong, you old goat." Jed nudged his friend to show he'd have none of his tomfoolery. "It's Homemade Holidays Down on the Homefront."

"Down Home Holidays Downtown," Josie jumped in to correct them both. Then she turned to Dora. "We thought, to generate some interest in people coming into town to eat and shop, we'd have a big kick-off celebration with a parade, street vendors and that evening a lighting ceremony and sing-along and maybe carriage rides through the street."

"That's what she's talking about," Jed proclaimed. "That's what she came for. Couldn't be nothing else, could it, Top Dawg?"

Burke cleared his throat. No lies. This did give them a position of strength. A reason for Dora to hang around. And he wanted her to hang around. For the work. Again he cleared his throat then nodded in her direction. "You really should stay. Give you a feel for the place like nothing else could."

Everyone looked at Dora as if her approval could make or break the whole event.

"I'd love to," Dora said, her eyes bright and her whole demeanor so light that Burke wanted to glance down to see if her feet had lifted off the ground.

"Great!" Josie approached as though she suddenly felt Dora were her personal guest. "Do you have a room at the motel or would you like to come out to the compound?"

The compound? Burke had asked her here to get a feel for the town, not to move in on his home turf. He frowned at her and maybe even shook his head, she wasn't sure.

Dora's shoulders slumped slightly, he thought, then rebounded and her standard straight arrow all-business poise returned.

"You didn't let me finish," she said. "I'd love to attend your Down Home Holidays Downtown."

She got it exactly right after hearing it only once. She would, of course, but it still impressed Burke and reminded him why she was the perfect person for the job.

"But I can't really stay around Mt. Knott indefinitely."

"Well, there's nothing indefinite about this, young lady," Jed noted.

"It's tomorrow night." Josie took her by the arm and began to lead her farther into the restaurant.

"A Tuesday?" Dora followed, her feet dragging slightly.

"No other time for it." Warren swung around to face the counter again.

"The Chamber of Commerce thought having it before Thanksgiving was rushing things a bit." Josie pointed to a seat at the counter for Dora.

Dora looked at Burke.

He smiled, though he suspected it wasn't a warm smile. If she wanted more, like some kind of affirmation that this was all a great idea, she wouldn't find it from him. Burke knew very little about any of this, seeing as he no longer played a role in the Chamber of Commerce, or in much of anything these days. He clenched his fingers and his jaw tightened at the reminder of all he had lost— all he no longer had to offer.

"And this past weekend, with people traveling to be with family and all, no sense in holding it then." Josie pulled a piece of green paper from beside the cash register and handed it to Dora.

"Not to mention that most any given Saturday half the town empties out, people heading elsewhere for shopping and entertainment and such." Jed stretched his neck out to peer over Dora's shoulder at the flyer with all the information about the event printed on it.

"Sunday is the Lord's day. Monday is get-back-to-work-and-already-realize-you're-a-day-behind day." Josie hurried to fetch another saucer and coffee cup. "Wednesday it's back to church for the goodly lot of us."

"Shouldn't that be the Godly lot of us?" Warren pondered aloud.

"Thursday's middle school football— we're in the play-offs." Josie set the saucer down and flipped the cup deftly. She nabbed the coffeepot and held it up to ask silently if Dora wanted any.

Dora nodded.

Josie poured. "Friday—high school football. That's an all-day and way into the night deal, what with pep rallies before and bonfires after."

"Then there we are back at Saturday and the great exodus." Jed nudged his own cup forward as if it were a reluctant volunteer that needed coaxing to step up and claim its refill.

"So Tuesday really was the only practical time to have it." Josie filled the cups, one right after another, with all the precision of a machine at the Crumble factory and a lot more grace and goodwill. She also saw to it that Jed and Warren each got another slice of pie, something no machine, or expense-conscious businesswoman, would ever have done.

"I see. Yes. I am interested in this." Dora waved the paper around in a way that made

Burke think that if it had been on white paper instead of green it would have looked like she intended to signal her complete surrender to the persistent and wonderful citizens of his hometown.

That thought made his hand freeze with his steaming cup of java halfway to his lips. Dora giving in to Mt. Knott? He never considered a thing like that could happen, but seeing her like this, all sweet expressions and hay in her hair, laughing at Jed and Warren's cornpone jokes?

"You know, if Ms. Hoag says she can't stay until the big event tomorrow night, we should probably just—"

"Do you suppose they have a vacancy at the hotel where I stayed last summer?" Dora pressed her lips tight and those big eyes of her went flinty and fixed on Burke's face. She crossed her arms and tipped her sweet, slightly pointed chin up.

He supposed that look had scared many a brave man, but it just made Burke want to grin. The woman had fire in her, he had to admit that.

"Then you'll stay for it." Josie clapped her hands.

But Burke had been burned too often and much too recently to dare to play with fire. "I'm sure Ms. Hoag is much too busy to...."

"I wasn't asking, Burke, I was insisting." And just that quickly Josie had Dora by the arm again, this time guiding her to the best booth in the place.

A booth. Not a seat at the counter. A seat at the counter said you were in a hurry, either that or you were Jed or Warren. But a booth? A booth said you were settling in for a spell.

Burke watched the women, then realized that everyone else was watching him watch them. Some curious, the rest sort of smug about seeing him overruled by his own sister-in-law.

Jed and Warren grinned.

"You are in big trouble now, boy," Jed muttered, swiveling around to go back to eating his pie.

"Half the town already got you married to that gal in their minds." Warren shook his head.

Burke knew they were right. Dora had walked in here a woman alone in the world and less than an hour later she was practically his fiancée. Only he didn't have a fiancée and wasn't looking for one.

This, he thought, mostly to himself but also a little bit as a plea for help to the Lord of all creation, this could be a problem.

Chapter Six

Dora's head was spinning. She couldn't figure this guy out. First, he hadn't wanted her to stay for Mt. Knott's Christmas kickoff. He'd asked her to come here but now he did not want her to stay. Why?

Dora glanced over her shoulder at the man standing with one hand on the lunch counter and the other raised to his forehead. A strand of blond hair fell across his knuckles, and he shook it off.

Jed or Warren—even though she'd spent many hours in this place last summer, Dora never had gotten straight which one was which—said something. Both men laughed. Burke's expression turned icy.

Dora plunked down in the seat and cradled

her coffee in both hands, though that did nothing to warm the chill she felt coming from Burke's blue eyes.

The man, Jed or Warren, had probably said something personal. Burke did not do personal.

But Mt. Knott and its residents? Nothing but personal. Too personal.

And personable.

They had taken Dora in today as if she had never left after last summer. They treated her like one of their very own. An old friend. No different from anyone, not even the town's Top Dawg.

To be treated like one of the crowd had to drive a man like Burke, a man who defined himself by his position, his accomplishments, crazy.

Dora smiled to herself. Mt. Knott might drive Burke crazy but she was just crazy about the place, and the people. She couldn't think of a nicer, warmer, sweeter place to be during the Christmas season, and she looked forward to the townwide event tomorrow night.

No, Burke did not want her here at all but here she was. She sighed.

She put her shoulders back against the seat

and drew in a deep breath, savoring the familiar smell of Josie's hearty fare.

Dora had eaten lunch at Josie's Home Cookin' Kitchen almost every day last summer. Sometimes dinner. Now and again breakfast. And coffee. Lots and lots of coffee at all hours of the day and night while she and Adam Burdett and Burke had pored over the details of the business, discussing what they should do, what they could do and what they would never want to do with it.

The thing they had never wanted to do was to let it slip out of family hands. Dora probably read too much into that, right up until the moment Burke had let her know she was never going to be a member of their family or their future business plans.

If it were possible, she felt even more unwanted by Burke now than she had sitting alone in her office on the day after Thanksgiving. What had she gotten herself into? And how did she get out?

She twisted around in the seat to look at the front door and the chalkboard wall caught her eye. Josie had painted almost an entire wall of the one-room restaurant with chalkboard paint to give the little ones something to occupy them while their parents visited with friends and ordered dessert.

Dora had to admire the younger woman's initiative and creativity. And, looking at how a portion of the wall had come to be used, she also had to admire Josie's heart. She'd allowed the townspeople to use the board to send messages, not just to each other, but in a special place sectioned off by vines and scrolled lettering, for prayer requests.

That section had been full last summer when many people had concerns about job security, the need for rain, the future of the Crumble. Dora fixed her gaze on the list now and shook her head.

The seasons had changed and, of course, the circumstances, but the things that people laid before the Lord varied little. Most people wanted the same things, after all, didn't they?

The sound of Burke's boots moving across the floor made her breath catch, but she kept on reading.

Prayers for health, well-being, peace of mind.

Prayers for prosperity.

Prayers for the people whom they loved.

People wanted to have a purpose, to have

enough to sustain them in that purpose and to love and be loved.

That's all Dora wanted, when you boiled it all down. Same as the folks in Mt. Knott. Same as everyone, even those who thought they were above all that mushy stuff.

The footsteps stopped.

Dora swung her head around at last and looked up at the king of the mushy-stuff haters. She smiled, even as the promise of tears bathed her eyes. "I can see why you chose here to start on the proj—"

"Pie." Burke interrupted with a stiffly cheerful insistence. He shifted his eyes, reminding her that they did not have the privacy here they would have had in a café in Atlanta. "Yeah, Josie makes great pie. Mind if I join you and we order ourselves some?"

"Yes, I…"

"You mind?" He actually looked disappointed.

"I mean, yes, I'd like some pie, and no, I don't mind if you join me." She motioned to the bench across from her in the booth. "But aren't you worried you're keeping me, since you seem to think I'm so busy I can't stick around until tomorrow night?"

"Yeah, about that, Dora." He dropped into the seat. "No hard feelings."

"Of course not. Nothing personal. Just business."

"Exactly." He nodded slowly then slumped back in the seat as though a great weight had been lifted from his shoulders. His broad shoulders strained at the denim of his work shirt, shoulders that looked like they could carry the weight of the world as easily as lift a small child to see tomorrow's Christmas parade. "Just business. I'm glad you said it and not me."

But you did say it! Had he forgotten already? Dora would never forget last summer, his hushed, hoarse voice, the clipped formality of his words, even the way he paused between one phrase and the next. *Nothing personal...just business.*

As if—well, she had never quite figured out why he had done that. Probably weighing his words so that he wouldn't give her anything to throw back at him.

Just like now. He'd let her use it as a justification for his actions, and how could she ever deride him for it? But it still hurt.

She tried to convey the message with her

eyes and with the tension in her body. With the silence she left hanging uncomfortably between them and finally by jabbing the toe of her shoe into his shin.

Which he did not even feel through his jeans and cowboy boots.

"As long as we're clear on that…." He jerked his chin up and looked toward the counter, searching.

"You thought I wasn't clear on that?" She batted her eyes, doling out a measure of unspoken sarcasm to go with her, well, big ol' dose of spoken sarcasm. Another message the big galoot did not pick up on.

"No, not you. I know you, Dora. You are all business."

Now there was a kick she couldn't ignore. She opened her mouth to protest that claim.

"Not…not all business." He made a face like a kid trying to fit together a complex model kit or do long division in his head. He brushed his hair back from where it touched the scar cutting across his darker blond eyebrow. "I know that. But as far as this business between us is concerned, you are. All business."

"Tell me once again about how you dazzle people with your charm?" She pursed her lips but couldn't hold it and broke into a subtle smile to let him know she was teasing.

He chuckled and caught Josie's attention and called out for two slices of her freshest pie.

"Going to take one out of the oven in a sec. Give it fifteen minutes to cool, and I'll have it right to you."

"Thanks." He checked his watch.

"Waiting for pie? Sounds like a good enough excuse for you to sit here, and I won't have to rush off back to my busy, busy life."

He had the good form to wince a little at his own behavior. But not much. "I said all that just now because I didn't want to appear too eager to have you here."

Dora's turn to wince. "Wow, thanks."

"You're welcome."

"How do you do that?"

"What?"

"Only hear what you want to hear."

"I wish. If I could do that I'd…" He looked into her eyes. He shook his head and looked away and said no more.

Unlike Burke, Dora had a knack for hearing both things said and those unsaid. It had come in handy in her line of work, but now it made her feel a bit too vulnerable. She did not know how she could keep things between her and Burke merely professional if he kept telling her so much about himself by not telling her anything.

She reached her hand out across the table. "You actually care what people here think of you?"

He looked down at the place where her hand rested near his. "No. Not so much. As the head of the town's biggest business, I couldn't let that kind of thing get to me."

She touched his wrist lightly with her fingertips.

"I don't care what anyone thinks." He withdrew and dropped his hand into his lap, shifting back in his seat. "But I do care about what people *say*."

"Spoken more like a VP of marketing, not a CEO," she teased. "But I thought there was no such thing as bad publicity."

He squinted, looked left then right, then focused in on her. "Dora, you don't know how people get ahold of an idea in a small town and run with it."

Now Dora took a look around them, her

eyes wide open. She observed the friendships all around them, the sense of community, the way that people wanted not only the best for themselves but for one another, too. She shook her head just a little and fixed her gaze on Burke again. "Actually, I suspect you are the one who doesn't know that, Burke."

"What do you mean?"

"Let's just say I don't think you are giving the people of Mt. Knott the credit they deserve."

"Yeah? Well, thanks to me and my lousy handling of the Crumble no one will give them the credit they deserve." He sat back, hearing what he wanted to hear all over again. "Going to be a bleak Christmas for a lot of folks around here, Dora."

"Money isn't the only thing that makes a merry Christmas, Burke," she said quite softly, since she doubted he'd listen.

He cast his eyes downward and nodded. "Yeah, but money is what I've got to give, thanks to my mom's life mission. Now you and I have to decide who to give it to."

"I can't help do that if you don't want me to stay here in Mt. Knott."

"I didn't mean for you to not actually stay,

Dora. I only felt I had to put up some resistance to your hanging around town."

She nodded. "To protect yourself."

"To protect you."

From what? *Humiliation*, he would have said and she knew it. Knew it because she had already lived through it once.

"Fair enough," she conceded. "You don't want people to know about, um, about our *business* or thinking they know too much about our personal lives."

"Yeah."

"Then why meet me here? Your sister-in-law's place is the social hub of the whole town."

"Nowhere else much to go on weekdays if you're retired or work second shift or are a farmer who doesn't have much to do this time of year."

Or are out of work because the Crumble laid you off, or a business dependent on people laid off by the Crumble closed. He didn't say it, but Dora only had to read the prayer requests on the chalkboard wall to know the thought had occurred to him.

"That and there's pie."

He smiled the most genuine smile she'd seen on him all day. "And there's pie."

"Good choice then." She pulled out a pad and pen and began to write. "Not to mention that the wall alone gives me enough information to keep me busy for days."

Burke's hand closed over hers. "What are you doing?"

"Making notes."

"You can't be seen doing that."

"Then how do I collect the information?"

He scowled and glanced around them. "You have a camera phone?"

She tapped the earpiece attached to the side of her head.

He studied her Bluetooth a moment. "Can you read them off, like into voice mail or something?"

"Or *you* could."

"What?"

"Pie!" Josie set down two plates in front of them with practiced stealth. "Won't bother you. If you need anything else, holler."

And she backed away. Didn't turn and walk away. Oh, no, backed away with her eyes on them the whole distance back to the counter.

Dora tried to hide a chuckle. Maybe Burke could control the things he said, but he had no sway over his friends and family. They would think what they liked and say what they thought.

Good for them.

Even if it would make her job—and maybe her holiday—a bit tougher.

"Where were we?" Burke asked, steadfastly ignoring the cherry pie filling that dripped from his raised fork.

"You were going to call and read the names to me so I wouldn't be caught writing them down."

He set the bite of pie down on the plate, his silverware clattering.

"Well, it makes sense, doesn't it? To me they are just names and a brief request," she said. "You should be able to give me more background."

From the look on his face, she realized he didn't think he could do that.

"Well, if you can give me anything more to go on, that would help." A sentence she had longed to say to this man time and time again over their brief courtship and at least a time or two since they had parted ways. *Give me something more to go on, help me to understand this.* Dora sighed. "If we want to keep up the appearance of my having come to town just to look around—"

"Which you did."

"Which I did." She took a bite of pie. It was as good as she remembered it. No, better. Maybe that was because she was enjoying the company. Or maybe because she was enjoying getting the best of that company. If Burke had wanted to call all the shots on this project he shouldn't have called in a corporate hotshot. "Then I should go and look. Poke around a bit. Maybe start with some churches, the library, the newspaper."

"And do what?"

She outlined the list, touching her fingers to count down the tasks she had in mind as she did. "Ask at the churches if there is anyone in need I could consider for a donation. Read up on the town as a whole and its history. Then, at the newspaper, maybe look up stories on past recipients."

He clasped his hand over her raised fingers to cut her off. "Those I have in my mom's files."

She cocked her head and smiled. She did

not slip her hand away from his. "Are you inviting me out to the Burdett compound to look them over?"

He let go of her hand. "No."

"Of course not." *Business. All business.* "Just as well, because I need you to stay here."

"Here?" He went for another bite of pie.

She gave him a look meant to scream, *you really do just hear what you want to hear,* and said, in a crisp, hushed voice, "To call me up and leave the names from the wall on my voice mail."

He wolfed down the bite. "Won't that look odd?"

"I thought you didn't care how you looked to other people?" Which was a shame because he looked terrific. Except for that…"You've got a…" She waved her hand over the side of her mouth. "Just a little…"

He frowned at her, confused.

"A…" Another wave of her hand. "Oh, here."

She stretched up from her seat, reached over the table and dabbed away a blob of bright red cherry filling from the corner of his mouth.

"Thanks." He laughed and swiped the pad of his thumb over the same spot. "Of course, now everyone in this diner is going to talk about this."

"About what a sloppy eater you are?" She sat back down.

"About how you and I shared some pie and how you found a reason to touch my face, to make it your business to look after me."

To make it your business to look after me. The thought made Dora sad and wistful all at once. "All the more reason for you to stay here and make the call. It will look better than the two of us heading out of here together."

"Good point. You certainly don't let anything slip by, Dora."

"Hey, what's a good little helper for?"

He looked at her a moment but said nothing.

A good helper. A helpmate. The thing she had always wanted so much to be for one man. For this man, she had once thought. Now she had her chance, even though it could not last.

"Hey, Josie, can I get a refill on coffee?" he called out, as if to remind Dora that in his world he had plenty of helpers. They were his employees, servers and beneficiaries. Though she had taken on this job strictly as a volunteer, he did not see her any differently.

"Anyway—" She started to slide out of the booth.

"Stay." He did not reach for her with anything but the most sincere look deep in his eyes.

Her heart stopped. She did not move.

"Wait until Josie gets over here, then we'll make our goodbyes. If we do it in the open like that it gives people less reason to try to guess what we said or why we said it."

She sat and felt her whole body sag a bit. "Funny, sometimes you can be right here hearing every word and still be left wondering those things."

"Hmm?"

"Eat your pie," she said. "We have a lot of work yet to do."

Chapter Seven

Burke could not read a single name on the list without stopping to wonder about the story behind the request. He knew some of them, but far too many held no larger meaning than they would for a stranger passing through town.

Conner Burdett had had a rule about knowing too much about the people who worked for him. He was against it. In much the same way kids learned in 4-H never to name the animals they later might have to sell for slaughter, the old man thought it best not to have any personal connection to a worker, because you might have to fire him later.

Adam, Josie's husband, the second Burdett

son, had followed that edict to the letter. Made him a better manager, some said. Most must have said it, Burke decided, since he was the man in change of the whole shebang now.

But Burke wasn't made that way. Despite being the adopted son, Adam was Conner all over. And Burke was his mother, in conscience, in commitment to a calling and by her design, now in Christmas spirit.

So where he had initially intended to pick and chose only the people most in need of some kind of grant, he ended up reading the entire list into the phone, each with a notation, a personal observation or bit of encouragement.

"The Sykes family asks for prayer for their daughter, Jenny, who is serving in the army overseas. Would be nice to do something for someone in the military."

And.

"The cheerleaders need to raise money to go to a competition this spring. It's not exactly what Mom had in mind, but I think it would give the whole town something to get behind. They need that. They deserve it."

And later:

"The Pennbreits simply say they are praying for everyone because it's all they can do right now. There's a story that would break your heart, Dora. I don't know if they have sons or daughters, though. Does it matter?"

He didn't think so but he trusted that Dora had the wherewithal and the detachment to make the right call on that. Still, he felt compelled to reminder her, "They're good folks. They're all good folks, Dora. I wish I had the means to help them all."

I know, but maybe you aren't meant to help them all, Burke, he could hear her soft words in her head. He could imagine her soft reply clearly in his mind. *Did you ever stop to think—*

"I am thinking, Dora. Can't help but think." He said out loud he'd meant that just as he had meant the last thing he said before flipping the phone shut and leaving the Home Cookin' Kitchen. "Guess sometimes you don't realize how blessed you are until you stop dwelling on all the wrongs you think have been done to you and look around at what other people are dealing with, and ask yourself, what can I do to make things better?"

What he had decided to do was head home. Yes, *home,* not the house, as he had taken to calling it since his mother had died.

Home. The place where he had grown up and where he had returned to live after his mother's death, for Conner's sake. As the oldest son and the one who had unseated the old man from his position as CEO of the company he had founded, it was Burke's duty to move back in. His place both as a son and as a brother. The only place he still retained now that Adam had taken over at the Crumble.

He sat in his truck and gazed at the house at the center of the Burdett compound. Five structures, each indicative of their owner.

Stray Dawg, the second son, the loner tamed by love who now had a wife, son and the reins of the business, had an upscale log cabin on a wooded two-acre lot. Jason, dubbed Lucky Dawg because he was born after Conner and Maggie had given up ever having another child and for never having broken a bone, despite a love of extreme sports, had designed an Irish cottage, complete with a meandering stone path and hunter-green shutters. While Cody, the youngest of the bunch, still called Hound Dawg despite having answered a call to the ministry, lived with his wife, Carol, in an old-fashioned-style farmhouse complete with wraparound front porch, like something right out of *The Andy Griffith Show.*

Burke's house, a small, simple ranch style, looked more like a guesthouse than a place where a man would want to spend his free time or one day raise his family. Dora had stayed there last year when she had been in negotiations to buy into the family business.

Burke had not even crossed its threshold since she had left. Not that they had happy memories there. She had always come over to the main house to avoid even the appearance of impropriety. But still, just knowing she had eaten breakfast at their table caught his imagination. She had rested her head on the pillows and dreamed who knows what dreams, about being his partner in life as well as business, he supposed. They had never discussed that eventuality outright but it had been an unspoken possibility that had woven itself through their every moment last summer. She had lived in his family's home, learned the ropes of his work, spent her days with his family. She had even attended Cody's church with him.

Home, work, family, church. She'd seen all the sides of the man that mattered and hadn't run off—until he had chased her off. It had humbled him then to think of a woman like Dora even considering caring for a man like him. Now? Well, now he wasn't that man anymore.

She must be counting her blessings today that she had escaped ending up with him. Here in South Carolina without a job or any real plans for the future.

Burke had invested his all in the company, in his place there and among his brothers, and his own family had sized him up and found him unworthy. Still, he had tried to fight for her. He had championed her cause of allowing her to buy into the Carolina Crumble Pattie Company and he had failed. He had been determined to get for Dora whatever she wanted one way or another, but in the end he had failed to get her a place in the business. The whole house of cards— home, work, family and all their unspoken possibilities—had caved in.

He gripped the steering wheel and gritted his teeth. By now she surely understood that she was better off without him.

He got out of the truck and stood, trying to decide whether to go to the main house where he had taken up residence—if by residence one meant that he had been sleeping on the pull-out sofa in his father's old office—or to finally return to his old house. The house he had once moved away from with a sure conviction of his station in life. The house that Dora had probably imagined the two of them would one day share.

He looked skyward for a moment, not seeking guidance from above, but just to find some respite from the choices laid out so plainly before him.

Following the brief flurries of Thanksgiving Day the temperature had warmed considerably. The clouds had cleared away. In fact, the sun shone so brightly that by nine in the morning people could shed their lightweight jackets. Everyone needed a baseball cap or dark glasses to shade their eyes, and here and there the summery sound of flip-flops could be heard along the sidewalks of Mt. Knott. In other words, the weather matched Burke's mood—totally inappropriate for the approaching holiday and the task that lay ahead for him.

There was only one way to change his mood. Something that he had to do, that he had promised Dora he would do. Something he had put off doing for two years now. He had to go to Santaland.

That made the choice of houses for him. In a matter of moments he was outside the locked doors of the attic office that no one had entered since his mother's death. Before that, only she had been allowed through those doors. Her office. Her sanctuary. Her domain. Right up until the night she had given him the key, told him what she had been doing all these years and to go and see it for himself.

He put his hand on the doorknob. He took a deep breath. Dust assaulted his nostrils. He sneezed. Once. Twice. Three times. Silly him, he half-expected to hear his mother's voice from the other side of the door call out, "God bless you, baby."

In the deafening silence that greeted him instead he thought better of the plan to come here. He turned, started to tuck the key away then paused. He sniffed, lightly this time, cautiously. What was that smell?

Pine. Probably from some scented candle that his mom had had on her desk to keep her in the holiday mood all year round. He imagined it, deep green in a large glass jar sitting right where she had placed it before she got too sick to climb the stairs.

It seemed to draw him back.

He had to do this.

For his mom.

For all the good folks of Mt. Knott.

For Dora.

"Dora," he said softly. He pulled his phone from his pocket, flipped it open and pressed the button to show his last placed call. If he were the kind to go in for a lot of heavy self-analysis, he'd say wanting to leave a message on Dora's voice mail at this precise moment was his way of not facing his memories and concerns all alone.

Instead he said out loud as he pushed Call, "I'll map the place out as I go so if she needs to get to files or anything I won't have to come back with her."

A soft electronic purring ring filled his ear.

He cranked the doorknob to the right and gave a nudge with the toe of his boot just above the threshold where age and weather had swollen the wood and made it stick.

Another ring.

The door swung open.

R-r-r-ring.

He flipped on the light.

Correction: Lights. Hundreds of them. Maybe thousands. Not just the two large overhead low-watt bulbs that glowed dimly from their frosted fixture-coverings, but string upon string of tiny twinklers strung from every rafter, framing every window and running along every surface. They even outlined the huge old desk painted gleaming black with bright gold scrollwork accents, in the same style as an old sleigh Burke's mother had purchased years ago and restored to perfection.

Guilt tugged at Burke over that. They had always stored the sleigh in the barn where they housed a couple of horses and countless cats. Each year when his mother had announced it was time to get the sleigh out and go caroling, Burke had been the one to go get it, hitch up the horse and bring it around.

That last year, the year his mother died, she had asked him to bring the sleigh out for her. "I want to give you boys one last happy memory."

"We don't want a memory, Mom. We want you to get better. You can't get better if you go out in the cold night air."

"Burke, I'm not going to get better. I certainly won't be well enough to go Christmas shopping this year. Memories are all I can give you this year."

Burke had refused.

Refused to fetch the sleigh. Refused to accept the memory-making experience. So a few days later when his mother had asked for another favor?

He glanced around him. From every nook and cranny statues, dolls and likenesses of Saint Nicholas peered out from under a robed hood, a red and white fur cap or even, in a couple instances, a cowboy hat.

"Take over my legacy, son. Continue the good work. Don't be afraid to change someone's life for the better."

When his mother had asked him to do this, he could not refuse.

Rr-r-r-r-ing.

The tone drew him into the present again. In a moment Dora's voice mail would pick up.

His gaze fell on the credenza behind the desk and all the framed photographs of the girls his mother's charity had helped over all these years.

All those stories. All those fresh starts and

new opportunities. All those changed lives. How had she chosen? How had she known who was deserving and how had she dealt with the disappointment that so few had given back to the cause?

That hadn't bothered her, he knew. She'd told him even at the end of her life that her responsibility was to be a cheerful giver and to act in the name of the Lord. She couldn't control what the receiver did after that. If they squandered their gifts or used them for ill, that would be between those receivers and God.

The lack of appreciation and failure to give back to the town was his issue. And one of the reasons he felt so inadequate to take this all on.

Maggie Burdett.

Saint Nicholas?

Top Dawg?

"Uh-uh." He pulled the phone away from his ear. There was one name he knew did not belong on that list and it was…

"Burke? Burke Burdett? Is that you?"

"Dora?"

"Don't sound so surprised. You called me."

"I thought I'd get your voice mail."

"You want me to hang up? You can call back and let my voice mail pick up."

Yes. That was exactly what he wanted. Oddly enough, it was also the one thing that he did not want—to lose contact with Dora. "That's kind of silly, isn't it?"

She didn't confirm or deny it.

"Yeah." He cleared his throat. "Okay. Well, I've got you now. That is, we have each other…on the line."

"Good. I actually found out a lot today and have some good leads. One thing I need your input on, though, is when to call the jeweler."

"The jeweler? Why?"

"It's the Christmas season, Burke, maybe not where you are but for the rest of us—"

"Oh, it's Christmas where I am." He shifted to take in the full panoramic view and chuckled. "Definitely Christmas."

"That's a busy time for a jeweler. We need to get our order in so he can have the charms ready and engraved with everything but the names of the recipients. I bet your mom had records about when she ordered them and all the specs on them."

"I'm sure she did." From the looks of it, his mom had never thrown anything away.

"Great. If you can just read them off to me?"

"Hold on. I'll just look over…here." He

tried to maneuver without tipping over tiny trees or stomping on delicate glass baubles. He yanked open a drawer only to find a small snow scene made from a mirror and cotton batting where file folders should have hung. "I'll tell you what. Why don't I handle everything with the jeweler?"

"Are you sure? I'll be headed back to Atlanta soon anyway."

"You will?" He shut the drawer with the snow scene in it and a puff of glitter sprayed up onto his hand. "Why?"

"Because that's where I live," she said, and left it at that.

Burke didn't need the lecture that could have followed. He thought she showed great restraint and good manners by not pointing out that he had left her little choice by not providing her a place to stay. "You can stay as long as you need to and bill your room at the motel to me, of course."

"What? I would never ask you to pay for that."

"You expect Global to pick up the tab when you travel. This is no different from that." He opened another drawer and then another searching for the information about the jeweler, or about his mother's selection system, or at least a tissue or hankie to clean the glitter from his hand. A dozen boxes of old-fashioned icicles tossed in with a ledger for the project, from a decade ago. Some tin noisemakers. The template for the letter she must have once meant to send with the coins but never finished. A sheet of self-adhesive gift tags. "Just a business expense. You may not take a salary for your time, but I can't let you pay out of your own pocket to help me do my job."

"Don't you mean your mission?"

"Do I?" He paused to give that a moment's thought.

"Or maybe a calling?"

Mission? Calling? The terms exuded a higher purpose than trying to assuage his guilt over his many failings. Burke couldn't own up to that. If he were to chose a word he'd pick *obligation. Responsibility.* An expectation that came with being born a Burdett. "No, *job* is the right word."

"Well, then I guess you're one of the lucky ones in Mt. Knott. Asking around all day I've heard that unless you work for the Crumble, there aren't any jobs to be had around here."

"How do you think I'd do at crumb cake inspecting?" The next drawer he tried stuck after opening only an inch. Were those files inside?

"I suspect you've known a few crumbs in your life," she shot back.

She didn't name names but he got the idea she meant him and felt it an unfair categorization. Instead of telling her so, though, he channeled his annoyance into freeing the stuck drawer and with one mighty tug.

"Christmas cards?" And not new ones that someone could use, either. But old ones, from people they hadn't known for years if they had known them at all, probably saved for the pretty pictures. "And speaking of pictures…"

"Were we speaking of pictures?"

Burke stared at the faded color photograph of him dressed as an elf for a kindergarten play. He chuckled under his breath. "Yeah. Yeah, we did speak about pictures. The one in my hand in particular."

"The…not the…the elf?"

He laughed at the unabashed delight in her voice. It was a sound he had heard almost daily during their summer together. He'd missed it. He'd missed her.

"Oh, this I have to see," she said. "Of course, I suspect to do that, I'd have to slide down the chimney by night and rifle through the house until I found it for myself."

"Actually—" He looked around, then at his hand, then at the boxes of junk and cabinets, also filled with junk. "You may be right."

"What? I, uh, Burke, I may be thin but I don't think I can actually fit down a chimney."

He chuckled.

"And as for rifling through a house? Not my bailiwick, buddy. Legal history, financial documents, tax records, ask me to find my way around those and I won't quit rummaging until I found out who owned the land the house sits on before Carolina was a state."

"That would be a Burdett," he informed her, half-wondering if he might turn up an ancestor or two in the dust and mayhem of his mother's office. "And that would be exactly the kind of dedication this situation calls for."

"Burdett dedication?"

"Dora dedication." He picked up a receipt for hundreds of dollars' worth of school supplies paperclipped to a pamphlet of illustrated Christmas carols. "The only way to get the information we need fast is to get someone to come to the house and organize my mother's things."

"I would be proud to help with that, Burke. All you have to do is—"

Ask. His mind went instantly to all those things left unsaid between them and he knew that if he did this, he had to be clear about what he wanted from her from the very start.

"You couldn't just come in and work up here in the office. No one else knows about this place. It's just a small space across the hall from where they think my mother used to spend her days." He wondered how anyone could have known his mother and believed that she could ever get anything done in the tidy yellow decoy room with the white furniture across the hall from her actual "office." "Whoever came in would have to pitch in and get the downstairs in order by day then work up here after hours when everyone thinks they have gone to bed."

Dora cleared her throat. "Is that a job offer, Mr. Burdett?"

"Well, it's not as glamorous a job as crumb inspector."

"Why would anyone believe I'd do that kind of thing—putting your mother's things in order—for you?"

"You wouldn't be doing it for *me*, really."

"No one would believe I was doing it for my health, now would they?"

"We'll tell them the truth. We needed an objective person to go through Mom's things but we also wanted someone familiar with the family. All we have to do is throw those two ideas out—a person who knows the Burdetts and can still be objective about us, and the list suddenly gets very narrow."

She hesitated.

He knew if he said anything more, asked her from his heart, gave just the tiniest insight into how much this meant to him, into what she meant to him, she would do it in an instant. And be hurt all the more when their work ended and she realized that he had nothing more to offer a woman like her. He remained silent.

She said nothing.

As negotiating tactics went, this was one of the oldest of the bunch. It went back to children in the school yard. First one to blink loses.

Finally, after what seemed forever, Dora sighed. "When do I start work?"

Burke tried not to sound too pleased with himself. "I'll move from the main house back into my old place in the morning. You can move in here anytime after noon tomorrow."

"Move in? I didn't really bring enough stuff to move in, Burke."

"You know what I mean."

"No, I don't. How long do you anticipate me staying?"

"Until the job's done."

"The job. Yes. Of course. Just business, huh?"

"Just business," he echoed. "Is there anything else?"

Tell me. Tell me, Dora, that there is something else.

She held her tongue for so long that he almost wondered if they had lost their connection. When she finally spoke he realized that their connection had been lost long before today, as she said in a quiet voice just before ending the call, "No, Burke. I guess there is nothing else. I guess maybe there never was."

Chapter Eight

Dora's heartbeat kicked up a notch. She'd come for the day, thinking she'd spend a few hours discussing things with Burke, gather what information she could then head back to Atlanta to sort through things. But here she was, already more than a day later, standing before the main house of the Burdett compound—moving in!

"Just visiting," she murmured firmly to keep that particular little flight of fancy in check. "No different than whatever five-star hotel I'd pick to spend the holidays in these last few years."

She gripped her purse and briefcase—she never went anywhere without it—in both hands, took a deep breath and marched up the front steps. She paused in front of the large door with its glass inset, looked down and saw four sets of footprints stenciled onto the painted floor. Hound Dawg's, the smallest, showed the treads of tennis shoes. Lucky Dawg, the name under the next set of prints preserved by a tough protective finish, had the feet positioned in such a way that Dora could almost see that brother's cocky stance. Adam, Stray Dawg's, prints faced toward the steps and the last set.

She moved to the full-sized boot prints, pointed directly at the door, of a man who knew where he belonged and had no intention of budging.

Dora looked around a moment. She wet her lips. She held her breath. This was it. Crossing the threshold back into the world she had once hoped would be hers meant…she didn't know what it meant, really, only that once she did this she couldn't undo it. Just like this past summer when she worked so closely with them—with Burke—she could only move through what happened next. No turning back.

If she were smart or, rather, wise, she'd run. She exhaled at last, looked straight ahead then stepped inside Burke's footprints.

They made her shoes look almost child-like. And though the footprints were only made of paint and many years old, she felt as though, through them, she had made a small connection to the man.

She put her hand on the doorknob and a shiver shot through her body.

Who was she kidding? No different than a five-star hotel? This was the Burdett family home.

The place where the man she had once hoped to have a future with was raised. Where he had lived these past two years. Where the people who had first invited her into their midst and into the middle of their business, then later tossed her out without so much as an explanation, met over deals and meals alike.

Dora reached out to touch two fingers to the ornate *B* etched in the glass of the oval inset on the dark green door.

"Five stars?" She looked at the grime on her fingertips then at the chipped paint around the broken brass and plastic doorbell, then at the footprints strangely preserved against the faded blue-gray of the weathered porch. "I don't think this place would even rate a lone star." She peered through the glass to the darkened rooms beyond. "A falling star, maybe."

At least at a hotel she got the hustle and bustle of holiday activity and a beautiful tree to gaze upon. Not to mention she usually enjoyed a roaring fire without having to go outside in the elements to gather wood. That and the lights and excitement of the city cheered her up.

Where were the Burdetts' decorations? The tree? The lights? What was there here to offer her a sense of warmth, of hope, of excitement?

The door swung open.

"Welcome to my home. It's good to have you here." Burke stepped up to the threshold, his hand extended.

Dora's arm trembled as her palm met his. Trembled! She had shaken hands with some of the most powerful people in her industry and never let her nerves get the better of her. Why couldn't she get control of herself now?

Burke's expression was an odd mix that Dora couldn't quite call delight but wouldn't deny held a certain amount of pleased relief. He was nervous, too. "I was beginning to think you'd changed your mind about coming."

She had changed her mind. Multiple times. Yet somehow it always got changed back and so here she was. Standing in Burke's shadow and in his footsteps. Giving up her usual holiday activities to give other people a Christmas while in return she would have—

She lost her train of thought as the smell of turkey and gravy, pumpkin pie and coffee filled the air.

"Dora's here!" Burke called over his shoulder.

"Don't make her stand outside, bring her in, we're waiting for her!" Josie peeked at her from the wide arching doorway that led to the dining room.

A cheer went up from the entire Burdett family.

She would give up her usual holiday and in return she would have the best shot at a real Christmas she'd ever known.

Dora came inside and before she could even thank them for welcoming her, Burke had taken her briefcase and someone else had scooped up the plastic bag of personal items she'd picked up at the one store in town, a chain discount, general mercantile type of place.

"Can we eat now?" Jason, the third of the dog pack, howled.

"Ain't fitting. T' have company like this fine lady come here and not provide her with a proper spread." Conner Burdett, who had probably once stood almost as tall as Burke, pushed his way past his sons and daughters-in-law. Rail thin and aged by grief, he still had a hard edge to him that said he wouldn't be taken advantage of.

Or fooled.

Or even charmed by anyone.

The grip of his handshake told Dora he recognized her as not just anyone. He knew who she was, what she did for a living and that in another place and time she would have been a powerful ally—or opponent—in business.

"Though I admit I find myself perplexed as to why you are here, Ms. Hoag. Why you would *want* to be here," he amended, his tone and demeanor changed from when he had barked at his wolf pack of a family.

Message received. Conner didn't want her here.

The old man turned and walked toward the arched doorway.

Dora shifted her gaze from one face to the next, ending with Burke. He prodded her to move with a nod of his head. Dora understood this as her cue to follow Conner and she did so.

"It's just leftovers, buffet style with these mangy mutts, nothing fancy," Burke warned her. "I hope that's okay."

"Okay?" Here was her out. She could simply say she thought she should find other accommodations, that an old house and Mt. Knott, South Carolina, simply did not meet her standards. Except…

She took a second to study those accommodations. The smiles, the smells, the light in the family's eyes and Burke, trying to smooth her way, and once again her mind changed.

"There a problem?" Conner demanded, turning slowly. "What's good enough for my kin not good enough for you, young woman?"

Dora eased out a long breath, brushed a glance Burke's way then met Conner's unyielding stance. "It's better than good enough, Mr. Burdett. Your home is grander and more agreeable than any five-star hotel in any exotic city in any corner of the world."

"What?" Conner turned and fixed a hard, squinty-eyed gaze on her. "What did you say?"

A lot of people would have been intimidated by the strange look on the old man's face and the energy with which he asked his question. Both seemed determined to push her back a step, knock her off balance, challenge her.

Obviously the man had not considered his target. If she did not know how to stand her ground, keep her equilibrium and rise to a challenge, she certainly would never have spent a day in the company of Burke Burdett. And she sure wouldn't be standing in his home now.

She raised her chin, trying to make herself an imposing figure, and smiled, because, well, the old man looked like he needed a kind smile. "I have traveled all over the world. Paris, Rome, Tokyo, I've stayed in fancy hotels and even a palace or two and I have to say, Mr. Burdett, your home has them all beat."

"You, little girl…" He stabbed a bony finger directly at her face.

She braced herself for a tirade, not sure if he would go into detail about everything he found lacking in her or merely call her a liar, which she wasn't.

Burke stepped up and put his arm around

her shoulders. "Mind your manners, old man."

"No, you mind yours. I'll remind you not to go grabbing on our honored guests like a crate of Crumble Patties ready for loading on a bakery truck." Conner plucked Burke's hand from Dora and batted it away.

"What?" Burke stepped back, his hands up, clearly more from surprise than from sheer obedience.

"Honored guest?" Dora asked.

"Why, yes." Conner beamed down at her and put his arm where Burke's had been moments before. "Such a perceptive, wise and well-spoken young lady, you are welcome in my home anytime."

"B-but don't you want to know why I'm here?"

"Yeah, you've come to put my house in order." Conner came off gruff but his pale eyes shone with gratitude and more than a little grief. That quickly shifted to something more like accusation as his attention went to Burke, then to impish sweetness as he turned to her and added, "And I couldn't think of another person on earth I would want to do it."

That shut Dora up.

At least long enough to try to take it all in.

"Seems a waste of a powerful executive." Adam, who had once worked under Dora's tutelage at Global and now ran the whole operation at the Crumble, eyed her cautiously.

Her cheeks burned. She had been so focused on her feelings about Burke that she hadn't thought about having to play the humble servant to people who had treated her so shabbily.

"But Burke said you volunteered," Adam went on. "He said you were the cheerful little helper type."

"Volun—? Cheerful little helper?" She shouldn't have been peeved by that and if it were just the two of them, she'd probably laugh off the whole elf connotation, but to let everyone think she'd pushed her way into this with such a flimsy excuse as being a helper type? This whole deal was Burke's doing and he needed to own up to some part in it. "I'd have never presumed to offer, of course, if Burke hadn't—"

"You know, I never even asked if you wanted to put your things away and clean up before we eat, Dora." Burke grabbed her by the elbow and pulled her gently against his chest.

At his touch, her anger faded more quickly than she would have liked. Anger, after all, had often proved a reliable ally in protecting her from people getting too close, and from any weakness on her part for trusting too much, too soon, too…"I'd like that."

As soon as they were out of earshot, she dug deep and tried to rekindle her initial feelings of embarrassment. "I volunteered?"

"What's wrong with that? Volunteering is nice."

"It makes me seem like I couldn't wait to worm my way back into…" Your heart. She struggled to take her eyes off him and tear her mind away from thoughts of what might have been between them. Maybe she shouldn't have come away alone with him, even just a flight of stairs or two. Even if it was all only a business proposition. That thought snapped her back to the reality of the situation. "It made me seem far too anxious to worm my way back into your family's good graces."

"Trust me, they would never even consider that was what you were doing."

"Because they see me as a serious professional?"

"Because..." He turned and winked at her over his shoulder. "My family is worm proof."

She opened her mouth to make a cutting remark about this not being the time for joking, then it dawned on her that he probably was not making a joke so much as a painful private observation and covering the truth of it with a joke. The Burdetts had shut him out as well as her, and it had to have left its mark on him. That concession was the most personal glimpse he'd given her into what was really going on with him these days. She accepted it, and his offering of closeness by opening up, with a gracious nod of her head.

He led her on upstairs, took her luggage and set it outside the door then beckoned her to a narrow doorway. It opened to a secluded stairway.

"Besides, I had to let them think it was your idea to see to my mother's things and that meant helping my father deal with her estate, because I couldn't very well tell them that this is why you had to come." He flipped on the light.

Dora gasped. No wonder they didn't have any exterior decorations. They were all here.

"Oh, Burke. You really are…"

"Don't call me that name."

"Name?"

"Jolly old you know who." He pressed one finger to her lips. "Please don't call me that. I'm just me. A flawed man without a clue how to accomplish the task before him."

His first concession about his family had been more than she expected from him. This uncustomary humility, this way of telling her how much he needed her without really telling her how much he needed her, this was a precious gift, indeed.

She closed her eyes and whispered, "No, you're not, you're the Top Dawg," placing her fingertips on his hand as he swept it along her cheek.

"Not any more." He shook his head. His hand fell away. "You saw it yourself. We're in my father's house. My brother speaks for the family and runs the Crumble. This is all I have."

"This seems quite enough, Burke. If you do the right things with it all." After a moment measured by no less than a heart-beat, it dawned on her she had said that while looking into his eyes.

He held her gaze for just one fleeting

second, then looked through the door, his jaw clenched. "It is what it is."

Just business. He did not say it, but he did say it, in his posture, in his grim expression even as he fixed his attention on the wonderful landscape of the office before them.

She flushed, cleared her throat then hastily flung her arm out toward the glittering space. "It's a great, um, jumping-off point."

"It's just a mishmash of an inheritance, not by my own doing. Plus I have to hide it away, which is not my style."

"Oh, I don't know. You seem a very private person to me." From *me,* she might have said instead but decided not to push it here and now. With her trust issues and all the things she had yet to say to him or his family about the way they had ended things, she was hardly one to throw stones.

"Yeah. I guess. But guarding your privacy and actually hiding things from people that matter to you? Very different. Doesn't feel right and yet…." He held his arms out to indicate the cluttered, covert office.

"Not your style."

He met her gaze and with an expression that admitted he was only half-kidding asked, "You think it's too late to change my nickname to Lost Dawg?"

"You're not lost. You can't be. You've always got someone to guide you." She reached down and picked up a multipointed silver star meant for the top of a Christmas tree.

He nodded then looked around at all the clutter of Christmas items overwhelming the small space. He rubbed his eyes and groaned. "I'm sorry I got you into this."

She set the star down and came to stand beside him. "I'm not."

His hands dropped from his face and he bent his head to look down into her eyes. "You're not?"

"I really do like it here," she whispered. She started to step back, literally moved by her own surprise at her confession, but Burke stopped her, taking her by the shoulders. She stilled and murmured, "I really, really like it."

"I like having you here."

"I'll try to be here every evening."

"What?" He cocked his head.

"In this office." She peered beyond him into the room. "I said I liked it here. You said you liked having me here. You did mean in the office, right?"

"No, Dora." He inched in closer.

"No?"

"I mean in my arms." He placed his crooked knuckles beneath her chin and nudged it up into just the right position to place a kiss on her waiting lips.

She wanted to tell him she couldn't allow that kind of overture. They were business associates, after all, nothing more. But in Burke's arms, kissing him, all that fell away. For the briefest measure of time, and despite the sparkle of Christmas ornaments and lights all around them, it was summer again. Anything was possible and—

"Dora? Burke? We went ahead and blessed the food. Served ourselves and now Jason wants to know if he can start on seconds or if he has to wait for you?" Adam's voice carried up the stairs and sliced between them as effectively as if he had pushed them apart and sent them to neutral corners.

Only Dora could not imagine a place in this house, in this town, in her heart or mind, where she would feel neutral about this man. That scared her.

A lot.

But fear alone could not account for the rabbit-quick beating of her heart.

"Sorry about that." He tipped his head to one side to make clear that he meant the interruption. "Hope having all these people around while you try to get things done doesn't drive you crazy."

"Are you kidding?" Dora embraced the chance to talk about anything that took the spotlight of awkwardness off what had just happened. "Spending time around your family is one of the reasons I came here. This will be the first Christmas in a very long time that I won't feel utterly alone in the world."

Quick thinking! Take the spotlight off how *readily you gave into his* kiss and put it right on the humiliating reminder that you have not a soul in the world who cares enough about you to share the most wonderful time of the year with you.

"Dora…"

He pitied her. She could tell. And she hated it.

Her whole life she had just wanted to give from her heart and find someone who would take what she had to offer gladly. People didn't take anything from those they pitied.

They became objects of sympathy and charity, not wellsprings from which to draw love and support.

Suddenly Dora realized that this might be the loneliest Christmas she'd ever known.

"We should go." Dora stepped backward and fussed with her hair.

"Yeah." Burke cleared his throat and jerked his thumb toward the open door. "By the way, I'll do whatever I can to help go through my mom's belongings downstairs for you."

"With me," she clarified, her head held high. "Expecting others to do the work I have committed to as mine is not my style."

Her clipped, driven business persona rose to the surface again.

"I know. That's why Global values you so much."

"Global? Values?" She tried to piece those words together so that they made sense to her but she just couldn't do it. Global was a huge corporation that thought of her as a cog in the machine. As long as she kept on churning and the wheels kept going round and round she had a job. The second she stopped? She harrumphed. "Where did you get the idea that Global cares anything about me?"

"You said they had been founded on Biblical principles." He repeated something she had told them when they had still been in discussions about the Carolina Crumble Pattie operation selling out to the megacorporation.

"Yes, a long, long time ago. They've grown. They've changed. They're no longer a family business, like yours."

"Hey, from where I'm standing mine's not strictly a family business anymore, either." He grumbled then he opened the door and held his hand out to allow her to go first.

The sounds of laughter, of plates clattering, of conversation wafted up from the lower story.

They washed over her, each one pricking at her raw emotions.

"That—" she pointed out the door, "—is not something I would ever hear at Global. Global is just a big, faceless and heartless corporation."

"That may be, but at least your heartless corporation hasn't kicked you to the curb. You don't see the faces at Global every time you get up in the morning and find you have nowhere to go. You still have a job."

Dora found it hard to feel sorry for Burke, who had so much, in contrast to her. She had, well, a job to do. "Speaking of jobs, when can I get back into this office?"

"My dad usually is asleep by nine."

"I can pitch in going through your mom's estate by day then, and come up here by night."

"I'd appreciate it. If you can make some sense out of her system that would help me next year and the year after and the year, when—"

"I get it." She cut him off because she did not want to hear the rest of that sentence.

"When you won't be around to help me anymore." He said it anyway.

"You just won't take a hint on a silver platter, will you?" She hurried past him and out into the hallway.

"Hmm? Hint? You mean—" He shut the door, turned the key in the lock then spun around and in one fluid movement snagged her arm and pulled her close. "This?"

"This is not a hint, Burke," she whispered, finding it hard to breathe. "This is either the real thing or nothing at all. It's not a game."

"Do I look like a man who plays games, Dora?"

"No." *Then kiss me again and make it*

mean something, she wanted to demand. Of course, she didn't. She wouldn't. A kiss like that from Burke was something he would have to give, his gift to her. And something he had to be willing to receive in return from her with the commitment that their kiss would mean more than a fleeting physical connection.

They had once had a future together, or more accurately, the promise of a future. That had changed and Dora did not completely understand why. But she was willing to try again. If he was.

He gazed deeply into her eyes.

She held her breath. Her heart pounded. She had no idea what he would do next.

"You're right." He let her arm go and moved away. "We can't let ourselves get distracted from the work ahead."

"Work," she said softly as she followed him down the stairs. "That *is* all there is between us, I guess."

"Did you say something?" he asked over his shoulder.

"I, um, I—" *If you can make some sense out of her system that would help me next year and the year after and the year, when you won't be around to help me anymore.* Burke had made his choice. She had to accept it.

They went down the stairs and headed for the dining room.

She should never have expected more. "I knew what I was getting into, Burke. I don't think you have to worry about me getting distracted again."

Chapter Nine

...This will be the first Christmas in a very long time that I won't feel utterly alone in the world.

Dora's words had kept coming back to him as they ate their meal, cleaned up afterwards, then all hurried off to the heart of Mt. Knott to join with the community to welcome in the coming season of goodwill.

"You know if it hadn't warmed up the way it has, I'd say drag out the old sleigh and ride into town," Jason announced, as they all headed for their cars outside their family home.

"Oh, I wish we could have." Carol turned to Cody, clapping her hands. "I only got to ride in it that one time. Of course, I'll never forget what happened that night."

"What happened that night?" Dora leaned in to whisper to Burke. "Did they get in an accident?"

Jason, who was passing by them at that very moment, barked out a laugh and promptly broke into the chorus of "Jingle Bells."

"Worse." Burke tried to maintain a proper scowl as he swung open the passenger door of his truck for his guest.

Dora put one hand on the door but did not climb up and into the cab right away, instead stopping to challenge him. He found that awfully charming, her fearlessness to stand up to him about the smallest things, even as a joke. "Worse?"

She clucked her tongue, shook her head and acted shocked to even imagine what could be worse.

"They got engaged," Burke answered, adding a jerk of his head to prod her to get into the car so they could get going and put this conversation behind them. He was not looking forward to having to spend his evening with the entire town of Mt. Knott, including a whole lot of people he had personally had to lay off from the Crumble. All of them acting as cheerful as possible. Trying to make it through the best they could. With him feeling guilty, both that he would be snooping around to decide which of them had the most pitiful circumstances, and that he could not simply help them all.

"Getting engaged is worse than getting into an accident?" she asked as he hurried her along.

"Doing anything that showy, like proposing in a sleigh, is worse because if you don't get it right or she turns you down, you will never hear the end of it."

"I can see that, especially in a small town like this where people are liable to talk," she agreed, joining in his jest.

"What do you two plan to get up to, to get people talking?" Cody asked, using his very most serious look of keeping an eye out for trouble, as any good preacher should.

"Nothing. Honest." Burke held his hands up like a kid who had been caught rattling the lid to the cookie jar. Then, for good measure, he gave Dora a quick wink. "We're on our best behavior."

"That's too bad," Conner grumbled, as he made his way slowly down the steps of the house, too proud to allow anyone to help him. "Don't know how this family is ever going to have any more grandkids with that kind of attitude."

Dora looked at Burke, a bit shocked.

"I'm not sure he actually heard what I said," Burke explained.

"Then again I'm not sure he didn't hear every syllable," Cody warned. Carol and Cody laughed, apparently having heard the old fellow's views about abandoning good sense and reason now and then in order to add a few new branches to the Burdett tree.

"Don't mind them. Sometimes they forget how to talk to people who aren't beholden to the Burdetts for their bread and butter." Burke stuck his hand out this time, trying to hurry her into the truck at last.

"I don't mind." She slipped her hand in his then paused for a moment. "I enjoyed sharing bread and butter with the Burdetts, so I guess I can stand it. In fact, I find it all endearing, the stories, the teasing and the bickering."

"I like her," Cody said, flashing the dimple that so many young women had sighed over that it had earned him the nickname Hound Dawg.

How could you argue with a woman who found your family's senseless babbling endearing? Went back to having spent so many holidays alone, he figured. Only explanation for finding charm in the Burdett clan. If only she had her own clan, her own relatives to laugh and bicker with.

"Anyway, it's not so bad getting talked about, you know." Cody gave Burke a playful punch in the arm.

Burke considered striking back, not hard but firmly enough to tell his baby brother he did not want a lecture on what he should do regarding Dora.

"After all," Cody went on, even before he dropped his fisted hand to his side. "Jesus was the talk of the town a time or too if you recall."

"Still is," Dora noted.

"So right," Cody nodded to her then gave Burke a no-nonsense look that suggested he thought his big brother should not let this woman go. "I'm telling ya, man, I like her."

"Maybe they should stay behind and rig up the sleigh." Carol whispered in her husband's ear loud enough for all to hear. She then wriggled the fingers of her left hand so that her diamond ring flashed in the light from the open truck cab. "Cody proposed to me in that sleigh on a winter's night three years ago."

"How romantic!" Dora folded her hands high on her chest and spoke directly to Cody. "Your idea?"

Cody pressed his lips tight and rolled his eyes in just the right way to silently rat out his older brother.

"You?" Dora looked at Burke with undisguised awe and surprise.

"Yeah. Well. I just—"

"Had to come from him." Conner passed his oldest son, clapping him hard on the shoulder as he did. "It's his sleigh. His mama bought it for him when he was a little tyke, before any of these other mangy mutts even came along."

Suddenly it dawned on him that his mother had been planning his taking over for her for a very long time. He'd certainly let her down these past two years.

Well, why not? Hadn't he let down everyone he cared about, as well as plenty of people he didn't even really know, these last two years?

"Your sleigh?" Dora cocked an eyebrow at Burke. "You own an actual sleigh? Is it red with gold trim and silver bells?"

He had cut her off before she could ask him where he kept his reindeer or make some other joke about the irony of the man who would rather not be Santa owning that particular kind of conveyance. "No. It's black and gold, just like—" Then he realized he had to cut himself off before he gave away where she would have seen the desk with the same high-gloss black paint and gold filigree. "Just like in an old Currier and Ives print."

"Oh, I'd love to see it sometime."

"Out in the barn." Cody helpfully pointed the way. "Though I can't for the life of me think of a reason he'd want to find an excuse to get you off alone in a dark, secluded place like that."

"I did ask if he'd put the wheels on it so we could take it into town tonight, maybe give some rides up and down Main Street and around the courthouse like the other people with wagons are doing," Josie chided, as she tucked her son into his car seat in the minivan parked next to Burke's truck.

"Guess he was too busy for that." Conner climbed into the seat beside his beloved grandson.

"I don't know doing what. Ain't like he

had to get up and go to a job like the rest of us." Adam tossed his car keys up and caught them again in the same hand.

"Maybe *busy* isn't the right word. *Distracted*. That's more like it." Cody, ever the peacemaker, rushed in to verbally separate the two older brothers, who seemed to have forever been warring with each other since Maggie and Conner had adopted Adam. Burke had seen him as not just a rival but a replacement.

"Right." Adam did not relent. He never did. He was like the old man that way, except he knew when to pick his battles. Adam didn't push the things that didn't need pushing. It was what made him the ideal candidate to run the newly reorganized business and made Burke want to grab him by the scruff of the neck and tell him to back off when Adam concluded, "Guess the man was too distracted by *something* to do the few things we depended on him to do."

In the past, Burke would have put his brothers in their places, or at least stood his ground to defend the scraps of his place in the family. Not today. Today, he had to try to digest the fact that his mother had been quietly asking him to take on this job his whole life and he had failed her. He had failed Josie with her simple request. Just as he had already failed Dora by not securing her investment in the Crumble—just as he'd surely fail her again if he let down his guard around her.

He caught a glimpse of Dora's face and the joy the exchange brought to her. He had failed her, but he would not do it again, starting here and now. These fleeting moments were all he could give her, after all.

"Yeah, yeah. You guys are just jealous because Mom bought you a car or a motorcycle, which none of you still owns, by the way, and she gave me a truly classic and classy mode of transportation."

"Because she knew you'd need it," Dora whispered.

He could not give her a home—his had been empty the last two years. Or a real job, the kind equal to her achievements. He had no idea what he would be doing once he'd fulfilled his obligation to follow through on his mother's pet project.

"At least once a year," she went on.

Beyond that…

There was no beyond that for them. Only the work before them. "Only this one Christmas," he reminded her.

"Then we should make it a memorable one," she murmured.

...the first Christmas in a very long time that I won't feel utterly alone in the world.

Burke understood how Dora felt. It was a cliché, Burke knew, that old saying about feeling alone in a crowd, but that didn't keep it from resonating deep within him.

A few minutes later, he looked out, mostly over the heads of the people milling around on the sidewalks of downtown Mt. Knott. People he had known his entire life, his family, his former employees, even his fifth-grade teacher, and yet Burke felt completely alone.

His gaze fell on Dora's sweet face.

Well, not completely.

What could he do to make this time memorable for her? To keep her from feeling the way he did now, deserted and misplaced, when her work here ended and she had to return to Atlanta alone for Christmas? Now that she'd heard about the sleigh-ride proposal—two things not on his agenda, marriage and sleigh rides—every small effort he might make would fall short.

"I don't think I've ever been to anything like this." She stood on tiptoe and made a sweeping search of the scene as if she feared missing something.

"Sure you have." He squinted at the clusters of people representing churches, schools, clubs and causes in town. The booths left over from the Fourth of July, done up in greenery and plastic red ribbon and candy canes, did seem a bit shabby and worn. "Well, maybe not *just* like this."

His mind went to the great decorations stored in the barn with the sleigh. He had worked a lot of hours organizing the outdoor lights with a system so that he could put them up single-handedly, because his brothers never seemed to be around when that kind of chore popped up. Of course, the best thing was the huge nativity scene, the kind usually seen in front of a church.

The figures were plaster casting that stood about three-quarters of a person's size. His mom had repainted their robes in vibrant colors to reflect the joy she felt for the occasion. It had always seemed gaudy to his tastes but people seemed to like to visit it set up on the courthouse lawn, until the year the town council got "nervous" about it and asked her to move it to the Crumble.

Instead she put it in crates in the barn and left it there. They hadn't been opened in ten years or more and now sat beneath tacky pink-and-blue-and-white sparkly fake fiber-optic trees, and three-foot-tall figures of Victorian carolers that rang bells when the right switch was flipped. He should have volunteered some of those things, not the nativity but other things to make this downtown festival a little brighter.

"So you did stick around, Miss Dora. Glad to have ya." Jed raised his whole arm and swung it back and forth in a greeting from across the way. "Too bad you couldn't get a handsomer date!"

"Someone's trying to get our attention." Dora gave a small wave back.

"That what he's doing?" Burke didn't mind that Jed found him unattractive, but the man did not have to go shouting things that made the whole town think he was Dora's date. "I thought maybe he was signaling to bring a small aircraft in for a landing."

"Small aircraft? Oh, you mean like a flying sleigh full of—*oof!*"

The gathering crowd pushed them closer together.

She put out her hand to brace herself from going face-first into his chest.

"Yeah, a sleigh full of *oof* and Saint Nicholas, too," he teased her softly, then bent his head and met her gaze. Just for a moment he knew they shared the same thought, the same memory—of the kiss that they shared.

Just this one Christmas. They should make it memorable.

She looked deeply into his eyes then broke contact and used her hand to steady herself. She smiled briefly then stepped away again.

They were wise not to follow through on another kiss. Still looking down at her now, he couldn't say the urge to pull her close had subsided so much as it had been subdued. It would be wrong, of course, to pursue a relationship with Dora at this point in his life. And he could not delude himself. If he kissed Dora again, with their already fragile history, he was as good as making a promise. A foundation from which the rest of their lives would be built.

It would imply trust and hope, things Dora clearly did not take lightly. Things that Burke would not offer lightly.

He fought the temptation to move still closer to her, to smell her hair, touch her face and see the light glow of a blush work across her cheeks. Then to lower his head and…

"Dunk the elf and win a prize!"

Burke blinked then looked around them again. The whole while he had been lost in Dora's eyes they had moved along with the cluster of people around them to the small midway of games and food booths.

All around them people laughed and greeted one another.

Overly loud Christmas music poured out of poorly placed speakers, crackling, crooning, then crackling again.

Adam and Josie had gone on into the Home Cookin' Kitchen leaving Conner to parade baby Nathan around, making sure nobody had any doubt as to the kid's lineage.

Carol and Cody met up with their youth group to check on proceedings at their Dunk the Elf booth. Some of the larger boys tried to convince Cody he should take a turn on the board above the murky tank of water.

"No one would dare dunk you, Preacher," someone called out.

"Ought to be *one* Burdett who'd step up and do it," came another observation.

"No," Burke said, before Dora could even open her mouth to volunteer him.

"I was going to suggest Adam," she shot back.

"Adam?" It should not have hurt his pride to hear that. But it did.

"He's the CEO. He's the guy they will take the most delight in soaking to raise money for the needy folks in town."

"Yeah, only he isn't the one who made them needy." He scanned the crowd knowing full well that this threadbare, makeshift gathering was going to be the highlight of more than one family's holiday, especially now that the Burdett party at the Crumble was a thing of the past. "I did that."

"No, your father did that. You tried to keep as many people employed as possible."

He looked at her, not sure whether to be impressed or wary.

"You have to know," she continued, "that I did plenty of research before I ever even considered investing in your company."

"Sure." He did know and just then it dawned on him that Adam probably had known, too. And Conner and the others. Could that have been behind the huge risk of not allowing Dora to buy in? She knew them too well, and she might have too readily stood with him against them.

Not that he saw his family as wicked or scheming. They had just come to one conclusion while Burke, and maybe Dora, had come to another. The other Burdetts were doing what they thought best, protecting the business they all loved just as much as he did.

It was one of those no-win situations, Burke thought. Only not winning had cost Dora and the townspeople more than it had any one of the Burdetts. Burke felt worse than ever now.

"Combing over the data, I believe your plan for the Crumble was working." Dora did not look at him as she spoke but strained her neck to get a good look at the goings-on in the church youth group booth. "Slowly. However, with a fresh infusion of cash things would have turned around soon."

"*Your* cash?"

She shrugged, still avoiding eye contact.

"I wish it had worked out that way," he said,

"So do I."

"Yeah?" He couldn't help smiling to think of her on his side.

At last she turned to him, her smile coy and a bit crooked. Her eyes glittered in the mix of streetlights and bright Christmas decorations. "If you had stayed in the top spot, it would be you on the board about to take the plunge right now."

For a split second Burke considered doing it, if just to show her he could take his lumps.

But before he could volunteer, Adam climbed into the seat and donned the baseball cap with the pointy ears that the kids had provided for him.

"Sure it wasn't your brother in that elf picture I've heard so much about? He looks awfully cute."

"I'm sure," Burke growled.

Carol took the first pitch and missed by a mile.

Cute? She thought Adam was cute? And for what? Doing the job Burke had done long before he got a shot at it? Taking the place in the business and in the dunking both that was rightfully Burke's? Dressing like an elf? Burke had done *that* long before Adam as well. "No. It's not Adam. It was my job long before he even came into the picture."

The crowd shouted for Carol to try again.

Adam laughed, put his thumbs in his ears, wiggled his hands and stuck out his tongue.

"What was your job?" Dora asked.

Carol cocked her arm back, placing the softball in perfect position—for Burke to take it.

"To be Top Dawg," Burke came back. He threw the ball with all his might at the small target.

Wham! The ball hit the mark.

Adam went down into the tank with a *yeowl,* his hat flying up in the air.

Some people whooped and started a chant, "Top Dawg! Top Dawg!"

Everybody laughed, even Adam.

Well, almost everybody. Burke couldn't shake Dora's assessment. It should have been him in that tank.

Not that he would have ever gotten in it.

He stared at his younger brother who rose from the water, dripping wet. He bent to pick up the cap he'd tossed to safety earlier and waved it to egg on the crowd.

Josie, standing ready with a towel, leaned

in to kiss Adam and found herself in a big, damp hug. She laughed, too.

The townspeople cheered some more.

Dora clapped.

For a fleeting moment everybody seemed content with their lives, happy even, and Burke had the odd sensation that maybe things were exactly as they should be.

Adam as the head of the business. The new leader of the Dawg pack.

"Isn't this a hoot?" Dora applauded Adam as he walked by, waving and enjoying the appreciation of the crowd.

"Oh yeah," Burke droned even as he found it in himself to give her a lopsided grin. "It's a regular hoot and a half."

"Be nice," she whispered.

"I am nice," he protested.

She narrowed her eyes, more flirting than challenging, and opened her mouth as if she had every intention of refuting his claim.

"Okay. You win a prize, Burke." Carol strolled up to them with a plastic mug with the church's name on it in one hand and a trio of glow-in-the-dark necklaces in other. "What do you want?"

He looked at Dora.

She mouthed the word *necklace* and, while he stored that preference away for future reference, he shook his head. "I want…"

Maybe it was the way he drawled it out. Or the fact that he spoke a bit too loud. That he stood a good five inches above the tallest person there. Or maybe, just maybe, it was because even after everything that had happened he really was still the Top Dawg— but everybody seemed to pause and listen.

"I want…" Burke nearly closed one eye and drew a bead on his younger brother. He pointed his finger. "I want his hat."

People whooped.

Dora beamed her approval.

"The hat isn't one of the prizes," Carol whispered.

Burke reached around to his back jeans pocket, tugged out his wallet, withdrew every last bit of cash he had on hand, tucked it all into the plastic mug in Carol's hand and said, "It is now."

"Give the man that hat, tank boy!" Cody demanded.

Adam obliged. Or rather, Josie obliged for him, giving it to Burke with a curtsy and a giggle.

Burke accepted it with a nod of his head then turned and presented it to Dora.

"This should come in handy," she said, giving it the once-over.

"I hope you don't already have one," he said, enjoying the look of excitement on her face. He helped her tuck her hair behind her ears and settle the hat on her head.

"How's it look?" She posed and batted her eyes for him.

"I don't know," he said softly.

She stopped still. "You don't know how my hat looks? Why not?"

"Because he's not looking at the hat," Jed called out.

And he wasn't.

He wanted now more than ever to kiss her. To make that promise.

"Okay, enough of this! Who's brave enough to go next?" Cody barked out.

Dora gave Burke a weak smile.

The younger brother pressed his hand to Burke's back to thank him for the donation and dunking Adam, and to prod him to take his obvious flirtation with Dora out of the church parking lot.

Burke moved on before Jed could make a

bad marriage pun about him and Dora taking the plunge.

"So, do you like that hat or not?" she asked again, clearly making nervous small talk.

"I like it." He wished now that he'd put that childhood picture of himself in his pocket and brought it to show her. "Reminds me of somebody I've seen a photo of lately."

"Don't see how it could." She walked ahead a few steps then turned to look at him over her shoulder. "I don't *have* anybody."

…the first Christmas in a very long time that I won't feel utterly alone in the world.

He couldn't give her much. Not a home or a position in the business or a future. But this? With a little help, maybe he could give her the one thing that would end her lonely Christmases from this year on.

Chapter Ten

The next week flew by faster for Dora than the final countdown of "The Twelve Days of Christmas" sung by a bunch of third-graders who knew that as soon as they finished the last *e-ee-e-eeee* of the partridge in a pear tree they'd be excused for cookies and punch.

During the daylight hours, Dora kept to the downstairs part of the family home, sifting through the remnants of Maggie Burdett's life. After a quiet dinner with Conner and sometimes Burke she would excuse herself and head upstairs, where she tried to sort out the remarkable woman's more private and encompassing legacy.

There was so much to learn about the town and its people. So many angles Dora could imagine taking to bring order to the eclectic mangle of a system Maggie had developed over the years. Should she consider granting the coins on merit or need or both? What about potential? Or doing the maximum good for the most people?

Would eight smaller gifts accomplish the goal? Or did it have to be one spectacular award to do Maggie Burdett justice? The only thing even resembling a mission statement Dora had found was what Burke had told her early on: *We give to others because God first gave Christ to us.*

All the while the days went whirling by. Those geese were a-layin', those swans a-swimmin' and those lords, Dora could practically feel those fancy-footed dudes doing a number on her poor aching head.

For the most part, Burke gave her no input. He always seemed to have mysterious work to do elsewhere or he just kept to himself in his ranch-style house sitting a half-acre away on the compound grounds. And yet everywhere that Dora looked she saw him, or something of him. And more often than not it gave her a glimpse into the man that his real and guarded presence never had.

She dragged her thoughts away from the man who had involved her in the project and then conveniently disappeared as she fixed on the task at hand.

"This single place setting doesn't seem to go with anything, Mr. Burdett." On her knees on the dining room floor, Dora held up a piece of china in a regal black-and-red pattern with gilded edging. With it she brandished a gold-plated knife, fork and spoon with clean, modern lines and a bold letter *B* engraved on the handles.

She carefully catalogued them on a yellow legal pad to leave a record so the often-squabbling siblings would know everything they came across and what had become of it. Often, while Conner Burdett told her the story of this thing or that, she doodled a quick sketch of an object or how she imagined it was used.

She flipped back to the first page of the pad to peek at the doodle there, a big shaggy dog wearing a Santa hat and elf ears. She considered drawing a Bad Dog sign beside the pooch and held back her smile as she turned again to the list and that troublesome lone place setting. "Should I box these up or put them with the things to give away?"

"Oh, no. No, no, no." Conner had dragged everything out of the linen closet and into the room, which was large enough to accommodate a long, dark table, eight straight-backed chairs, a buffet, a china cabinet and still leave room for a person to move all the way around with a serving cart. He held his hand up. "Don't go and do either of those things."

Dora took a deep breath and braced herself to hear what Conner had said about every scrap of paper, piece of clothing or useless nicknack she had held up— "There's a story behind that." Which he would then proceed to tell her.

At length.

In detail.

Twice.

"No, no, no." He shook his head, squinting. "Put those back in the china cabinet where you found them."

Dora waited for more.

Conner went back to shuffling through a stack of tablecloths.

Maybe he hadn't understood her question. Or perhaps in the dim light from the dingy, aging crystal chandelier, he hadn't actually seen what she had held up. "Mr. Burdett?"

"Now how many times have I asked you to call me Conner?" He gave her a sly smile and then a wink. "Mr. Burdett is my first-born."

Dora had to chuckle at that, even though she completely understood and agreed with the comment. "Conner, then. I…"

"Look here." He yanked up a crisp pink, white and olive-green cloth with a motif of funky Santas and Christmas greetings in odd-size text. "Maggie got this the very first Christmas after we began keeping company." Conner, sitting in the chair at the head of the table, unfolded one corner then practically caressed the cloth with the palm of his weathered hand. "Before we were married, or even engaged yet."

"For her hope chest?" Dora wondered aloud. Her great-aunt had had one of those and tried to start one for Dora, who had told her that none of the other girls Dora's age had one. The truth was that Dora would have loved one but the last thing she needed was yet another thing to single her out, make her seem out of touch.

"Hope chest?" Conner scratched his head. "No. Not for my Maggie. Her hopes ran in an entirely different direction than tablecloths and putting away things for home and hearth. That's why when she showed me this, I knew."

Dora leaned in to get a closer look. "Knew what?"

"That she was going to be my wife."

Upon closer inspection the tablecloth made her almost laugh out loud. She couldn't imagine old sour Burke growing up eating Christmas dinner off this.

"I had just about given up the whole idea that Maggie would want to settle down and stay here in Mt. Knott with me. But this tablecloth changed all that. Perfect fit for this table, which had belonged to my parents."

"Let's keep it out, then." She accepted the cloth from his hands as though it were made of spun gold. "I'll launder and press it and we can put it on the table for Christmas in honor of your marriage and your Maggie."

"Thank you, Dora, for doing this with me." His eyes got misty, for only a second, then he cleared his throat. "You're the only person in these past two years would have trusted with the task."

"Me? But Mr, um, Conner, you really

hardly know me and what you do know, well, I got the impression, no, actually, the legal notice of failure to complete a contract that made it pretty clear your family didn't really have much use for me."

That was the sore spot. All her life Dora had found her niche in being useful. To be told she wasn't?

"That were the case you wouldn't be here now, would you?" He scoffed and went back to sorting through the other tablecloths, hardly able to hide the tears welling in his eyes with each memory they brought.

"I see" she murmured, humbled at the freshness of the man's grief even now.

There was so much sadness in this house, so much gone unsaid between family members that might have healed it, or lessened it. It made Dora's heart ache for them. Was it really so hard, she wondered, this relationship between parent and child?

She shook her head and went back to the work at hand. "But this? Why would you want to keep a single place setting?"

"It's Burke's."

"Burke's?" She held it up. It was hardly big enough to serve a slice of Josie's pie and had no companion pieces. "Burke has a china pattern?"

"It was his when he was a baby."

"Baby? But it's fine china."

"Nothing but the best for my son."

"So they each have one?" She looked up and tried to find three more plates with utensils.

"No. Just Burke. Just our little prince."

"Your Top Dawg," she said softly.

"From the day he was born," Conner confirmed. "By the time we adopted Adam we had figured out how impractical it was, feeding boys off fancy plates."

"Guess Burke taught you a thing or two." She smiled.

"In his own way, yes."

"And what way was that?" she asked.

"The hard way, my dear." He said with a gleam in his eye and unabashed pride in his voice. "Always the hard way."

Dora laughed, but not from the heart. Her thoughts went back to trying to teach herself how to run the Forgotten Stocking Project and her head throbbed anew. "I'm surprised this plate survived intact."

"I ain't rightly sure he ever used it." The older man reached out and took the plate for his own inspection. "But, oh, the plans we had for that boy when we bought it and then…."

"Then you realized he had plans of his own," she said softly. Suddenly the parent/child conflict became clearer in her mind. What, she wondered, had Conner expected of Burke that he could not give?

Giving, she realized in that instant, was not Burke's strong suit. And giving was the only thing a parent would want, that a child not act grudgingly or out of teeth-gritting obedience but to submit freely and from the heart. Yes. She could imagine the conflict between father and son now, and had a new insight into the reasons the Bible often taught about the relationship with God in terms of a loving Father wanting the best for His children.

"For I know the plans I have laid for you," declares the Lord, "plans to prosper you and not harm you, plans to give you hope and a future." Being a lifelong planner who always feared for her own future, Jeremiah 29, verse 11 had always held a special appeal for Dora.

"That's nice." Conner folded his hands and gazed at the plate again. "That's all I ever wanted for my sons. For them to prosper. For them to have hope and a good future."

"You provided for that, Conner, when you built up the family business."

"Exactly why I did it." He nodded, still not making eye contact with her. "And exactly why I didn't think—don't think—all of my boys should carry on in it."

Wow. What an odd and yet profound statement. The kind of thing Dora suspected the old man might never have said to anyone else. The kind of thing she wanted to hear more about. "Are you saying—"

"I'm saying this work won't do itself." He clapped his hands. "We still got a week's worth of work ahead, and that's not taking into account the barn or the upstairs."

"Week? Barn? Upstairs?" She didn't know which to worry about first. She had planned to head back to Atlanta in a couple of days. She hoped that distance and her own surroundings would help her gain perspective on the best approach for the project. "I don't think I can stay out here doing this for that long. I have things that need my attention."

He trained a beady eye on her. "You were a jiggler, weren't you?"

"A—" Dora didn't know whether to be insulted or charmed. "What?"

"When you were little. I bet you were the one who crept in under the cover of darkness, laid on your belly under the Christmas tree and gave each and every one of your presents a little—" He raised both hands as if holding a package then demonstrated as he said, "—a jiggle."

Dora laughed and hoped it didn't come off too awkward and iffy. "No, Mr. Bur—"

"Eh, eh, eh."

"Conner. I was not then nor have I ever been a jiggler."

"Of course not." Burke leaned in, plucked up the yellow legal pad and began glancing over it as he said, "Way too unreliable a means of checking inventory for our Dora."

"How long have you been standing there—" She turned away from Burke, leaning against the doorframe with a heart-melting smile on his lips, to his father as she shared an inside joke with the older of the two men, *"Mr. Burdett?"*

Another of the brothers would have naturally protested that Mr. Burdett was their father. Given the old man his props, as it were.

Not Burke. Not Mr. Business. Not the real *Mr. Burdett.*

He wasn't going to give anybody anything. Not even a direct answer.

"Where you been?" Conner wanted to know.

"I had things to do," he said cryptically.

"Apparently you didn't get them all done." Conner dove back into the work before him.

"What makes you say that?" Burke asked.

"You forgot to pick up dinner."

Every evening since she had gotten here Burke had shown up about this time with "to go" boxes from Josie's restaurant. The food was good and plentiful and Dora hadn't minded one bit not having to add cooking to her list of duties. But she had felt a bit strange that it probably looked to Conner as if she were too snobby to pitch in and pull together a simple meal.

"I'll go back to town in a minute," Burke said. "How are things going here?"

"We found your baby plate."

"Can't say you ever ate off it." Conner gazed at it and whispered, "But, oh what plans we had…."

"I don't see any use in keeping it." Burke handed her the legal pad, pointing to the plate listing, as if to order her to move it off the list of keepers.

Dora took a breath but did not take the pad, not just yet. Taking it implied agreeing with him and she couldn't do that as long as Burke would not even give his father a moment of sentimentality. She wanted to—well, never mind what she wanted, she decided, reining in the temptation to lose her temper or to cross the line between personal and professional behavior. Burke wouldn't give anything, including a hoot about what his father was really saying to him.

"Bad dog," she muttered under her breath.

"What?" Burke pushed the pad toward her again and when he did the pages flipped to reveal the drawing on the front.

He paused, studied the blatant representation of himself with elf ears and finally chuckled softly before handing it to her again. "I'll go back to town to pick up dinner now. Is the special okay with everyone?"

This time she did take the pad. Maybe the man wasn't so bad.

Dora had already given plenty, but then she had come here looking for a way to give as much of herself as possible. Maybe that meant she needed to set an example and give a little more. "How about I do the cooking tonight?"

She worked her way over toward Conner on her knees, intent on using the arm of his chair to climb to her feet.

As she wriggled by, Burke nabbed her by the arm and helped her up, peering down into her eyes with a hint of doubt as he asked, "You cook?"

"I sure do." She freed her arm from his grasp and tipped up her nose. "When there's a fridge full of Josie's wonderful leftovers to throw together into a casserole or hash."

"Oh. Yeah? Well, in that case, I cook, too," he shot back with a grin, showing a glimpse of the man who had assured her that he was actually this nice at the downtown holiday event.

"Then maybe you should give us all a break and do the honors tonight," she teased. Only she wasn't completely teasing. She honestly thought it would serve this man well—this high-born prince of snack-cake bakers, this sometimes very bad dog—to do some good for others instead of deciding for them or directing them or even dogging them.

Of course, that was the part he picked up on. The kernel of truth beneath the jest. Dora should have seen that coming. It's exactly what she would have done, only she liked to think she'd arrive at a more accurate reason to have taken offense at the remark.

"I should cook because I'm the only one who hasn't been working?" Burke still had her hand in his, and his hurt and anger held her attention as though they were alone in the room. "Is that what you're saying?"

"No." *Well, sort of.* She had, if she confessed, been aiming to change him, because she thought he could do more, be more. She had no business prodding him that way, of course.

Because the only thing between them *was* business.

"Just laying out the terms of the contract, Mr. Burdett. You know, always ask for more than you think the other guy will ever give when you begin negotiations." A smart tactic usually but since Burke wasn't about to give anything, just opening her mouth had blown the whole deal at the onset. "We have leftovers and both of us are equally capable of—"

"I submit that capability in cooking is a pretty subjective thing, Ms. Hoag," he shifted quite easily into CEO mode.

Something that did not put her off one bit. "I gladly accept your submission, Mr. Burdett, and I—"

"Knock it off, the pair of you!" Conner moved the table linens from his lap to the floor, signaling the end of his task and his patience. "You both know how to cook. The kitchen is thataway. I'm hungry."

Burke and Dora exchanged a brief look. In a boardroom, they probably would have shaken hands as a sign that they had reached an agreement. Instead they started off in the direction Conner had just pointed.

"Good. Go. About time you two turned up the heat." Conner waved them away, calling after them. "And while you're at it, make some dinner, too!"

"I'm sorry about him," Burke said as he ushered her into the kitchen.

"Don't be. I like him." She went to the fridge and started pulling out the remnants of earlier meals.

"Well, he likes you, too."

"You say that like you think we both have bad taste in the company we keep."

"Did I?" He frowned but she wasn't sure that it was a comment on how she had read him, or because the food in the container he had just opened had gone bad.

So she went on, getting out a big ceramic casserole dish and pulling salt and pepper from the overhead cabinet. She knew where it all was, having gone through this room cataloging every gadget and gewgaw.

As she worked she made the kind of small talk she usually heard other people making in the break room. A question couched as a thought. A tidbit of information thrown out for comment without the formality of requesting a comment or opinion. "Um, your dad thinks we have a week's worth of work left but I think I should go back to Atlanta for a few days."

"I agree." He threw the box he'd just sniffed into the trash can.

"With what?" This was why she never engaged in that break room chitchat. She wasn't any good at it. And, of course, everyone at work was so afraid of her they usually emptied the room before she could attempt to join the conversation. "Staying for another week or going back to Atlanta?"

"Atlanta." He scanned the boxes and picked up another one. A quick peek inside then he handed it to her. "Start with this."

She took the box and peered inside, too, feeling more like part of a production line than a participant in a conversation or creative endeavor. "Okay. Then what?"

"Then you tell me where I can meet you there."

She'd meant *then what do I add to the mix of leftovers?* not *then what happens with you and me?* "You and me? In Atlanta? At the same time?"

"Sure."

She clutched a wooden spoon in her hand until her knuckles went white. Maybe she had read him all wrong. Maybe he was more giving than she thought and right now he was giving her a chance to make something more of their relationship. "In Atlanta?"

"If that's where you'll be, then that's where I need to be."

She stopped filling a casserole dish with macaroni and cheese from the box Burke had passed to her. How long had she waited to hear him say just that? She took a step toward him.

"Yeah. Makes sense doesn't it?" Another box, this time set aside. "Down there we don't have to have any secrets."

"Secrets? About the project?"

"About the…Oh! Yes, the project. Yes. That's right. How could I forget the project? It's the reason I'm here. I do have a lot to talk to you about." She flipped the last of the boxes open and studied the contents. "We need something to hold all this together."

"The project?"

"The food, you know, some canned cream-of-anything soup?" Dora jerked her head up. Actually, yes, that was exactly what they needed for the project, something to hold it, and them, together long enough to see it through. "Now that you mention it, though, we do need something to make this project cohesive. It's all over the place now. I can't seem to find any formula for how your mom made her choices. If we—"

"Save it." He plunked down a can with a pull-top lid then made a stirring motion with one hand to ask her to hand him the spoon. "In Atlanta we can meet someplace, you can give me your report and answer any questions I have then."

"Ok," she murmured, as the glop from the can fell on top of the noodles with a slurpy plop. She had come here because she thought she had something to give, but in reality what she had given had always been his to begin with, his to take and his to reject if he so desired.

She slapped the spoon into his palm, not angrily but more like a nurse handing a surgeon a scalpel. They would be in Atlanta just what they were here and now, a couple of professionals with a deadline on a job they had both committed to see through. "Then after that I can go over things with the accountant and get an order in with the jeweler."

"I'll do that." He stepped in and took over the construction of the casserole as well.

"I don't mind." She held her hands up, feeling absolutely useless. Her least favorite feeling in the world.

She watched him a moment and realized that he had already begun to pull away from her, the way one does when a collaboration nears conclusion. *Correction,* she thought, *feeling useless is my* second *least favorite feeling in the world.*

He churned the food in the dish and added salt and pepper, never once turning to acknowledge her. "Dealing with the other team members, that's my place, Dora."

And she had just been put in hers.

"Besides, if you and I are both gone at the same time then we both return at the same time, people will talk." He yanked open a cabinet, pulled out a half-empty bag of potato chips and sprinkled some on top of the mix. "I won't have that."

She leaned back against the counter, trying to get some satisfaction from the fact that he had taken over the meal-prep duties after all. "Protecting your reputation, eh?"

"Protecting yours."

"Gallant but unnecessary." Just how she felt about him taking charge of the kitchen instead of offering to do it out of kindness and generosity. "I don't care what people think of me if I know my actions are honorable and right."

"Yes, but you're working in my home. And though people don't know it, on my mother's project. I can't have that compromised."

Right. Business. It always came back to that with him. Everything did. She suspected that after the Christmas festival he had made his brother write out a charitable donation receipt with a notation at the bottom: For elf employment.

"So, Atlanta?" he asked.

"Atlanta." She nodded then suggested a place for them to meet.

"I'll put it on my calendar." He slid the casserole into the oven and set the timer.

"Me, too," she said, watching him walk away, leaving her with the less glam job of cleaning up the small mess they had made.

She looked around her. She was spending her yearly vacation in an old house in Mt. Knott, South Carolina, playing helper to the world's surliest Santa.

This was her gift, not to Burke, but to the town, and now to dear, still-grieving Conner Burdett and to Maggie. They deserved her best.

Come to think of it, *she* deserved her best.

She was going to do this the way she would if it were her project from the get-go. Then she would find a way to bring it all together and when they met in Atlanta she would give her all to Burke with no strings, no expectations and, like that fellow who sent the rings, the hens, the drummers, dancers and maids a-milking, a strict no-givebacks policy.

Chapter Eleven

"Job hunting? That was your story?" Dora slid into the back booth in the small coffee shop at the address she had given him to meet her. "You told your family you were off job hunting?"

"Sure? Why not?" And by that Burke meant, *why not do a little job hunting* as much as, *why not tell the family that's what I'm doing?* He took the other side of the booth, making the table wobble with every inch he scooted along the shiny-red vinyl and gray duct tape–patched bench. "Nice place you picked to meet, by the way."

"I like it." Dora pulled her laptop from its case, flipped it open. "It's quiet, out of the way."

He checked out the clientele, more of a

"can't never tell" lot, it seemed to him. A couple of bleary-eyed types with one hand affixed to a computer and a coffee cup in the other. And in the corner a fellow who clearly felt invisible to the world, and liked it that way. "Yeah, the place is practically abandoned."

"Hey, it has ambiance." She connected her Wi-Fi service with the push of a button.

"Good. I think people who eat here sometimes *need* an ambulance."

"Ambiance. Atmosphere. It's cozy. Quaint. A piece of Americana. One of those, what's the word?"

"A dive?"

"A mom-and-pop operation," she corrected with a hint of a smile and a steely-eyed glower.

Mom-and-pop. Suddenly he understood the appeal it had for a woman who had neither. So he tried to find something positive to say about the place where Dora had practically set up an office away from, well, her office. "I see they have a bottomless cup of coffee."

He pointed to a sign, smiling, trying to make nice.

She barely took her eyes off the computer screen.

Forget nice, he wanted to see the fire in her eyes. "Of course they don't say if that means they keep refilling your drink, or if the coffee is so strong it eats the bottom right out of the cup."

That did it. She gave him the look, all flash and polish and a touch of little girl ready to defend her corner of the playground.

"I like their coffee," she said.

I like you, Burke wanted to say. Instead he just sighed and shook his head, grinning like a fool.

That softened her up a bit and she conceded, "So the place is a bit of a greasy spoon."

"I don't think the grease is limited to the spoons, Dora." He picked up his water glass and held it up so that the fluorescent light shone through, highlighting the smudges.

"Enough of that. So, it's no Josie's Home Cookin' Kitchen—"

"Or Dora's home cooking for that matter." He meant that as a jab at his having come all the way to Atlanta to meet with her and her not inviting him to her home, but she didn't seem to pick up on that.

"But it's got big tables where they won't

chase you off if you sit for a while, a Wi-Fi hotspot and the coffee keeps coming."

Or maybe she had brought him to the place where she spent more time than home. "Spoken like a woman who comes here often."

"Not *that* often."

"Hey, Dora. The usual?" A chubby-cheeked waitress in a bib apron with the strings wrapped around her thick middle and tied in front—which gave her a soft, lumpy look that seemed to say "hey, the food's great here"—offered up a half-empty coffeepot.

"No, thanks." Dora put her hand over the top of her coffee cup and glanced nervously at the waitress. "I, uh, think I'll have hot chocolate."

"Hot chocolate? Really? This early in the—"

"No time of day too early for hot chocolate." Dora beamed.

"—Season," the waitress finished. "I mean you don't normally switch to the sweet stuff until the week before Christmas."

"What can I say? I'm in a holiday mood," Dora droned, her beam decidedly bummed.

"Last year you held off right up until Christmas Eve. Or was it two years ago?"

Dora blanched.

Burke loved it.

And hated it.

Loved seeing her squirm like this, getting this tiny glimpse into her secret indulgence of hot chocolate around the holidays, but hated, hated, hated the thought of this bright-eyed, brilliant woman spending Christmas Eve in this greasy spoon. Granted, he could see what drew her to the mom-and-pop operation but he couldn't help thinking that even Mom and Pop found something better to do on December twenty-fourth than hang around here.

"And for you, sir? Hot chocolate as well? It's good. I can highly recommend it."

Burke scowled. "I don't usually go for the—"

"He's already so sweet as it is," Dora needled.

"I was going to say I don't usually go for the rich stuff."

"He rich enough as it is?" The waitress didn't so much as smirk to apologize for the directness of her question.

"As a matter of fact..." Dora gave him a look.

"I'll take the hot chocolate," he said.

"With a shot of Dairy Dream on top?" she asked, pointing to a laminated picture clipped to the menu of a frothy whipped-creamlike substance floating on a cup.

Dora opened her mouth but Burke cut her off. Much as he'd love to hear her say out loud that he was, indeed, *dreamy* enough already, he actually wanted the stuff in his drink. "That would be fine. Thank you."

The waitress snapped a very professional "Yes sir" and scooted off, calling out after herself, "I'll bring your whipped cream in a dish on the side, Dora, just like always."

"Don't come here that often, eh?"

Dora bit her lower lip and raised her shoulders sheepishly as she gave Burke a guilty glance.

He would have gloated at being proven right so eloquently, so unarguably, so…deliciously, except that seeing her like this he didn't feel like gloating.

"Shall we get down to work? Or do you have to rush off and put in your application someplace?" She whipped her head around toward the front door. "Hey, you know, I think I might have seen a Now Hiring sign in the window here. If you want I can put in a good word for you."

He shifted awkwardly and the cushion beneath him sighed and groaned. "Yeah, I want to talk to you about that."

"About the work we need to do or about your claim that you are job hunting?"

"Can't I do both?"

"Oh, Burke, really. You have such a noble cause to tend to." She sat up all prim and proper in her navy-blue business suit and gleaming but simple gold jewelry.

Suddenly he wished he had chosen the glow-in-the-dark necklaces as his prize at the church dunking-booth. He'd have loved to see her in those, and the elf hat, and.... "Excuse me, did you say noble cause?"

"Your mother's legacy." She rolled her eyes, something he figured she'd never do in a bona fide business meeting, and pressed on, "I don't believe for one second you want to do anything, especially anything as demanding as job hunting, to distract you from that right now. Or ever."

"Ever? A man has to work, Dora."

"And there is plenty of work to be done with this, Burke." She slapped down a stack of file folders onto the table even as her eyes fixed on the computer screen. "I can see why your mother worked on it year-round. It's a full-time job in its own right. Or could be. If you did it right."

If you did it right. The reminder that he had not done it, or much of anything, right stung. Suddenly the thought of asking her to put in a good word for him at Global seemed pointless. Silly, even. Besides, Adam had worked at Global. Burke was looking to blaze his own trail once again, as he always had, not to follow in his younger brother's footsteps. But the job interview he'd had there this afternoon had gone so well, and the position they had open sounded like a perfect fit for him.

His teeth were on edge. He wanted to defend his work ethic and record to her on one hand, but, on the other, she had offered him the single best hope for doing something meaningful with his life since his family had so lightly dismissed him. Between a rock and a hard place. Only there was nothing hard about Dora, though many people thought of her as tough as nails. He saw right through that to the little girl all alone in the world, and to that scared and lonely child all he could say was, "I'm listening."

"I've been thinking a lot about this." She scooted forward, her eyes lit with enthusiasm. "You could create a foundation to build on your mother's dream."

"I think my mother has already laid a pretty good foundation, Dora."

"Not that kind of foundation, Burke. This kind." She pressed a button on her keyboard and spun her laptop around.

There, on the screen was a logo, a hand-sketched image of the coin that his mother had made at the jewelers in Atlanta with a glimmer of light bouncing off the rim. Below it, in simple but elegant script, the words *The Forgotten Stocking Foundation.*

He pointed to it. "What's this?"

"Just a rough example. I toyed with the idea of a stocking or a something more, oh, you know, Santa-ish, but then I thought it was a better idea to honor the One who moved the original Saint Nicholas and us to action." She stroked her fingertip over the upper right curve of the coin on the screen.

Burke blinked and when his eyes focused in he realized what he had taken to be a flash to show the shine of the gold was really the image of the cross at the center of a star of Bethlehem.

He nodded slowly. He liked it. "But I don't really understand it."

"Your mom accomplished so much, Burke, but in a way that only a person who lived and worked and listened and learned about the goings-on and needs of a small community could."

The waitress brought their hot chocolates and clunked them down, the cups clattering against the saucers, the saucers thumping against the table. She opened her mouth to say something but Burke spoke first.

"Go on." He'd meant to encourage Dora to keep talking but the waitress must have taken it as a direct command, and she hurried off.

"Maggie did so much."

"You said that."

"But—" She wet her lips.

"I thought so." He sat back. "She did so much but what? She didn't do enough?"

"I'm not criticizing her, Burke. I'm not trying to downplay any of the work she did."

"But?"

"Just looking over the records I have been able to pull together, I am in awe of her." She placed her hand on a thick file folder. "She helped so many people, created the recipe and the logo for the Carolina Crumble Pattie and raised four very competent and compassionate sons."

"But?" He was a Dawg with a bone.

"But I think we could do more. Much more."

We? She had no right to include herself in his family business. No more place in it than he did. And he guessed, in a funny way, that did make them a *we*. "What makes you think *we* need to do more?"

"See for yourself." She worked a second file from beneath the first one and slid it across the table toward him.

"More rough examples?"

"No. More harsh realities."

He frowned then flipped open the file folder to see a name along with a page full of neatly typed notes on the person's situation. He picked that up and beneath it found another name, another summation. And under that another and another. He raised his gaze to meet Dora's.

She sighed and tugged a piece of paper

from the pile. "Look here. A budding scientist who can't go away to college because her mother died last year and there are two younger siblings to care for."

"I know them."

"A talented painter who just needs a little space for a studio."

He nodded at the name on the page. "She's good."

"A family who—"

He put his hand down over the page she was peering at. "Dora. I know all this. I know there are a lot of worthy folks in need, that's why I hired you to sort them out."

"Sort them how, Burke? By depth of desperation? By the most potential good to be seen, and if that, whose good and over how long? Does someone who can be a doctor take precedence over someone who wants to go to a technical school and be at work in six months? Does the scientist get a coin while the artist gets an empty stocking?"

He looked again at the papers lying side by side and shook his head. "Maybe we could do both."

"Maybe so but we can't do all of them."

Now he got it. Now he saw her quandary.

"Let me guess, you want to help all of them, don't you, Dora?"

She didn't say yes, but she didn't have to because it shone in her kind eyes and the way she pressed her lips tightly together to keep from blurting out something totally unprofessional.

"Dora, I don't see how—"

"I thought you'd never ask."

With that she launched into what Burke could only call a high-powered, take-no-prisoners, this-was-why-Global-paid-her-the-big-bucks-and-gave-her-a-company-car, smokin' sales pitch for the establishment of the Maggie Burdett Forgotten Stocking Foundation.

It sounded great.

Correction. Her voice sounded great.

"This year we make the announcement and give small grants with multiple recipients. What we can't do we ask locals to pitch in and help with. Someone probably has empty space for that studio, and surely someone can help with day care for those kids if we pay for reliable transportation so the college-bound girl can come back and forth on weekends."

Her *enthusiasm* sounded great.

"Then the real work begins. First we set up the means to raise money to serve just the immediate region. In a year or so the whole state. Eventually we should be able to reach anywhere they know the name Carolina Crumble Pattie."

Even the way she paused and took the tiniest sip of hot chocolate then smacked her lips ever so slightly sounded great. The pitch? Burke really wasn't listening.

He didn't have to listen.

"It sounds good, Dora."

"I'm so glad you think so. When can we—"

"Never."

"Never?"

His brothers and father had displaced him, and he did not owe them anything. The town had all but forgotten his years of dedication and sacrifice in favor of the promise of a new start with Adam, while they themselves made no effort to invest in Mt. Knott or one another. He owed them even less. He had made promises to Dora and to his mother— those he would honor but even they had their limits. Or, rather, he had his limits. He did not have it in him to do what Dora was asking.

"Just this one Christmas, Dora. That's all I committed to. That's all I have in me."

"But why? You sat right here a few minutes ago and told me you were ready to take on a new job."

"I am." He flipped the file folder in front of him closed. "I plan to take a job, too. I feel that I have a lot to give if someone would have me."

I'll have you.

She'd never say it. She didn't want him any more than anyone did, he supposed, but he would give her ample opportunity to prove him wrong. When she sat there, her eyes narrowed and her lips pressed tight, he went on. "As soon as this one Christmas is past, I will be back hard at work again, but not as Santa Claus to the entire South."

"So you're rejecting this out of hand?"

"No, I'm rejecting it out of common sense."

Her face went pale. Her lower lip quivered so slightly he doubted anyone else would have noticed it. Then she rallied and raised her chin. The disappointment in her eyes cleared. She nodded. "I see."

"Look, Dora, it's not personal. It's just—"

She held her hand up. "As an early Christmas present to me, I'm going to ask that you not finish that sentence."

He shut his mouth. Nodded once.

She nodded, too. Then forced a mild, tense smile and nodded again.

For a few minutes he felt that they might sit there like that for the rest of the night, like two silent bobble-head dolls. Nodding and smiling. Nodding and smiling.

In his capacity as CEO, this was the point where he would have stood up, shaken her hand and thanked her for her time before walking away. Nice and tidy. But today he was acting as a person, talking with another person, dealing with feelings and history and…and nothing about it was nice or tidy.

Well, last summer had been nice right up until the part when his whole world fell apart. He flexed his hands around the mug of hot chocolate and tried to think what more he could say. "So, how do you plan to spend the rest of the day?"

"Foundation or not, the job isn't done."

He reached for the files. "I can take it from here."

"I mean the job I'm doing for your father.

I owe it to him to see that through until the end."

"You're going to Mt. Knott?" He hadn't expected that.

"Don't worry. I'll try to finish up before you get back." She clicked her laptop shut, tucked it in the case and slid out of the booth. "That will be my Christmas present to you."

Chapter Twelve

Dora stood in the dining room of the main Burdett house, trying to look inconspicuous while three brothers and two wives finally faced the mountain of memories left by their mother. Burke had not returned from Atlanta nor had they seen one another after their tiff in the coffee shop.

She'd given it her best shot and been turned down. Only business, she reminded herself, nothing personal.

Her part was over. In reality she probably should have excused herself and gone upstairs to finish up there. But she really didn't think she could manage that without drawing attention to Maggie's secret office and the project that she had kept hidden from the family her whole marriage.

Families. Dora didn't know what to think of them. Of this one, at least. Her own, she had always believed was the exception to all the rules.

"What was Christmas like when the boys were young, Conner?" She asked a unifying question to try to make herself useful.

"A lot of grabbing and arguing and pushing and pulling, and a lot of laughter and love. Basically just like every other day around here."

"Hey! That's mine." The next to the youngest brother, Jason, lunged for an old tin box, the kind Boy Scouts used to sell filled with peanut brittle or log candy at fund-raiser time. Dora had found a whole stash of the things in the back of a closet, most of them empty but a few holding the kinds of treasures young boys might have stowed inside—marbles, rocks, four-leaf clovers.

"No, yours was red." Cody held the box up high, just out of reach from the brother a scant year older, but a full four inches shorter. "This one, the blue one, is mine."

"You're both wrong." Adam, the eldest,

and shortest, of the three, leapt up and whisked the box away from the grasping fingers of his younger siblings. "That's mine. I know because I left a dent in the underside of it when I banged Burke over the head with it when he said it was his."

"Ha! That proves it can't be yours. If this metal had ever met with Burke's hard head it would be dented beyond repair," Jason observed.

To which the other brothers paused, shared a look, then broke into laugher.

Adam turned the box over in his hands. "Bet Burke still has his tin squirreled away someplace. Man, you can't get that dog to turn lose of anything."

He'd turned lose of her pretty easily, Dora thought before it dawned on her. Maybe he never really had ahold of her—maybe the connection she felt last summer had come from her alone?

"Hey, like we don't know that." Jason eyed the tin as if he weren't quite sure he was ready to let Adam keep it. "Hasn't forgiven us yet for ousting him from the Crumble."

"I still feel pretty lousy about that," Cody confessed.

Dora tensed. She wondered if she should excuse herself, or start humming Christmas carols really loudly to remind them they had an interloper in the midst. Except, she really wanted to hear this.

"Don't none of you try to carry the burden for that decision." Conner pulled himself up to his full height for the first time since Dora had been here. He set his jaw in grim determination, but kindness and care flickered in his eyes. "That was strictly my doing."

"Yours?" It slipped out before Dora's decorum could lock it inside her.

"Yes, young lady. Me and that firstborn of mine been at odds since long before I decided he ought to eat off fine china."

She looked once again to the plate.

"He's the one you thought shouldn't follow you into the family business?"

Conner's mouth twitched. He gave his other sons a once-over then he turned to her. "Too much of his mother in him. Too much of the little prince we expected him to be. Both those things always at war inside him."

That's why the old man kept that place setting. It wasn't just a reminder of the plans he had for Burke but of how he had tried to shape his son into something he wasn't meant to be and the price they had both paid. The conflict between them, the things he felt he had robbed his son of doing.

"So you corrected that by kicking him out of the business?" she asked.

"We had words. We had legal battles. We even came to blows at one point. But in the end I bested him with the one thing I knew he'd have to accept—good business."

Dora tried to take all that in. "Is that why you turned my investment down?"

"Didn't seem right to invite you into the family just when we kicked Burke out." Cody gave a sympathetic shrug.

"Personally, I was all for that." Adam threw his hands up to show he had no part in her rejection. "You would be way more nice to sit across from in board meetings."

"Prettier, too," Jason agreed.

Dora had to smile at that even while she had no idea what to do with the rest of the information. "Have you ever told Burke any of this?"

"Did she suggest trying to reason with Tog Dawg?" Adam asked, laughing.

"Reason he'd go for, like telling him we were doing it for his own good? He'd pull an

Adam just to prove us wrong." Cody gave his
older brother, the one who had run off with
his inheritance and taken a job with Global
to try to run the family out of business, a jab
in the ribs with his elbow.

"Neither the business nor the family could
have withstood that," Conner told her.

"Hate to contradict you, sir." She folded
her arms and looked at the lot of them. "But
I've gone over your business with a fine-
tooth comb and seen the inner workings of
your family and I have to say both are far
stronger than you are giving them credit for."

"Flattery ain't going to change our minds,"
Adam tossed the tin in his hand up a few
inches and caught it again.

"Yeah, if you want to be a part of the
business or the family, you're going to have
to do it the old-fashioned way," Cody
warned.

"Hostile takeover?" she asked, one eyebrow cocked.

"Some might call it that." Conner
chuckled. "But we were thinking if you want
to be one of this pack, you're going to have
to marry into it."

With that they all dove back into the once

neatly stacked piles of things that Dora had spent days going through and organizing to see what they wanted to keep, store away for future generations or give away.

Marry? It wasn't even within the realm of possibility. Dora knew that, but why ruin this shot at making a lasting memory with something so impermanent as reality?

Boxes got shuffled from hand to hand. Papers avalanched onto the floor. Grown men whooped like children at coming across some long forgotten memento.

"Some things never change." Conner chuckled softly.

"Some things have changed, though. A lot." Dora moved her gaze away from the undoing of all her hard work to the closet where she had relegated box upon box of Christmas decorations, filling the small storage closet from floor to ceiling. "I take it you once went all out with the decorations."

Conner followed her line of vision. "We haven't had any of that stuff up since we lost our sweet Maggie. She passed at Christmastime, you know."

"I know." Dora put her hand on the old man's arm. "It must be hard for you to see all those things. If you'd like I'll just shut the door and leave them for you to deal with another time."

"But?" He stopped her in her tracks.

She inhaled and held it, then let it out with a soft chuckle. "Did anyone ever tell you that you sound a lot like Burke?"

The man's forehead wrinkled in confusion.

Dora laughed.

"I guess maybe the real issue is that the men of this family have no difficulty reading me like a book. They don't just hear what I say, they listen to what I am *not* saying." Dora looked from Conner to Adam then to the single place setting she had carefully, some might say lovingly, placed front and center in the china cabinet, the one that had been for Burke. "And unlike the people who work for me, they have the gumption to call me on it."

Conner had seen through her lame attempt to suggest that it was time to return to their old family traditions. Adam had stayed ahead of her in business negotiations and sent her packing before she had known what hit her. And Burke?

Being a master of not having to say much to speak volumes, Burke had seen through the razzle-dazzle of her Forgotten Stocking Foundation to the heart of the matter. She had tried to horn in on his territory. To make herself a part of his work, his family and his life.

Dora wet her lips. "Okay, you got me. I could close that closet door and leave it all for you to deal with at some later date. To let another Christmas go by without a tree or any lights or even a manger scene that I suspect your wife would have set up in a prominent place year after year."

"You know about that? We haven't set that thing up in more than a decade."

"You haven't had a crèche in your home for that long?"

"A crèche? Oh, no. I thought you meant the near life-size one we used to set up for the whole town."

"You have a nearly life-size nativity scene?" She whipped around to look at the boxes, sure she wouldn't have missed *that*.

"We did. Not too sure what became of it after Maggie had a meltdown over the town council kicking the holy family off the courthouse lawn, though. Burke might know. His mama always went to him to deal with things like that."

Dora chose not to respond to that, out of respect for Maggie and the objective of keeping secret what Maggie had asked Burke to deal with.

"There is a smaller crèche in there someplace though. She picked it up on some island. Can't recall which—" His face contorted with the strain of trying to remember.

"Fiji? Hawaii? Crete?"

"Long!" He snapped his fingers.

"Long Island?"

"Got it at a dime store. Little plastic thing." He made a frame with his hands to indicate the size. "Got it before she even met me and said she always dreamt of starting a collection of nativities from everyplace she traveled. Wanted a whole roomful but then she met me and ended up with just the two— the big one and that plastic thing. Not enough to even fill a box."

"What she ended up with could not be contained by even this one house," Dora reminded him, and with a hand on his shoulder, drew his attention back to Adam and Josie with their son, Nathan, to Cody, Carol and Jason, all talking at once, holding up objects and sharing their fondest feelings about their mom.

Conner smiled at last. "I reckon you think it's time to let some of what she loved spill out again?"

"I do."

"What do you have in mind?"

She hadn't actually gotten Burke a Christmas gift besides her promise to leave before he returned. Which she still planned to do but somehow, after all they had shared, she felt she should do more. No, it was more than that.

She still saw so much good in Burke. So much, well, as much as she had tried to avoid the emotion her whole life, *hope*. He had so much to give if he would only let go of it. So much to share. Not with her, she understood that. He felt undone by the loss of his job, his lifelong work, his place at the top. He associated her with that loss, and she, of all people, understood that.

But he had brought her here to give something that only she could. She had yet to do that. The work on the project? He could have hired someone else, someone who had no contact at all with the town or the workers at the Crumble or his family, to compile all that and even make recommendations for him. What he could not appoint anyone else in the world to do was to tell him the truth.

She owed that to him. And he owed her... one memorable Christmas.

"Well, we have all these things and the house is so drab...."

And just like that Dora found herself in the middle of a family. Not an outsider. Not an observer. A member.

They heard her out then flew into a decorating frenzy. The sisters-in-law worked on the inside of the house, hanging swags of faux pine with red-and-gold ribbon over the fireplace and around the banister and filling every empty space with nicknacks and baubles. The brothers tackled the outside. That didn't take as long as Dora had expected since a whole system of hooks and latches that were hardly visible during the year had been installed and the lights, which had all been stored in neat rolls with tags showing where they went, fit right into them.

She and Conner took on setting up the

large artificial, pre-lit tree and had just finished putting the star on the top when the doorbell rang.

Dora gasped. "I didn't think Burke would come back for another hour or more."

"Burke? Since when does he ring the doorbell?" Josie asked, even as she hurried to answer it.

"We three kings…" the three Burdett brothers belted out their own version of the old song, this one extolling their hard work and success at outdoor holiday lighting.

The women laughed.

Conner joined them. They stepped out onto the porch and, as the final note of the song warbled through the rafters, Adam flipped a switch.

"Oh!"

"Wow!"

"You did all this?"

A thousand white lights twinkled around them, warming the dusky late-afternoon sky like candles lighting the way on an overcast day. Framed by a semicircle of glittering pastel trees set of Victorian-style carolers stood, some moving mechanically from left to right, others lowering and raising song-books and all of them opening and closing their mouths silently.

Cody pointed to them and laughed, sheepishly. "We couldn't find the music but Burke just drove up so we can ask—"

"Who did this?"

"Burke?" Dora stepped from behind Conner, her heart pounding. She had wanted to do this for him and be gone, to leave him with this wonderful sight and never see him again. But here he was.

Here *she* was.

And here was her heart, laid out and exposed in this small token she had wanted Burke to have—his family Christmas restored to him. "I planned to leave before now but it all took a little longer than I expected."

"So this was your doing?" he responded in quick, barely controlled anger.

Indifference. Mild amusement. Even gratitude, those she might have anticipated. But anger? Why anger?

The old Dora, the woman she had been before spending these last two weeks going over other people's troubles, thinking of ways to be of service, acting in a small way as a part of a family and a community, would have seen this coming. That Dora knew to never let your heart or your hopes do the work of your history or your head. "It was my idea, yes, but I only wanted to help."

He shook his head and anger faded to something else. Pain? Embarrassment? "If I need help, I hire it."

"You hired me to help," she reminded him.

"Not anymore." He moved past her, then looked back. Framed in the glow and flicker of thousands of lights, he fixed his eyes on her alone, angled his chin up and set his jaw as he said, quietly, "You're fired."

Chapter Thirteen

"Fired? Fired? I'll tell you who is fired, mister. You. You are the one who is fired here. I should have known you wouldn't be up to the job."

"Burke was working for Dora?"

Dora and Burke both startled at hearing Adam's voice. They looked his way then at the rest of the family staring unashamedly at them.

"I am not working for anyone, least of all you, Adam. Or any Burdett. That means I don't owe a one of you an explanation." Burke nabbed Dora by the arm and pulled her, gently but firmly, into the house.

She cooperated and went with him but the second they crossed the threshold, she yanked her arm free.

The door fell shut.

Dora turned on Burke, her eyes flashing. "Unlike your family, I may not have the power to actually fire you from the work we're doing, Burke, but somebody should. Someone as stubborn and prideful as you has no business setting himself up as some kind of icon of giving during the most joyous season of the year."

He stepped back. He'd come home thinking he'd find things much as he had left them, without decorations and without Dora. Instead he had returned to find all the people who had shirked the duty of decorating the house for their mother standing around congratulating themselves on a job well done— using his system. And now Dora was standing here telling him he didn't belong in the only role he had left?

Actually, that he sort of agreed with, in principle, if not in the personal emotional toll it would take. "Hey, I never wanted that job in the first place."

"Good, it doesn't suit you." She snapped. This time when her lower lip quivered she did not control it well. Tears glittered in her eyes. The little girl who he had always known lurked just beneath the surface of her unflappable, businesslike exterior came out of hiding and in full temper-tantrum mode to boot. "In fact, you'd look pretty silly in the suit that comes with the job, anyway."

That hurt. It shouldn't have. After all, what she'd told him was he couldn't pull off the jolly old elf look in red, fur and jingle bells. No rosy cheeks. No snowy white beard. No belly like a bowlful of jelly for him, no sir. In a way it was a compliment.

Only Dora didn't mean it as a compliment. And that bugged him.

The fact that it bugged him, well, that scared him. Because it meant that deep down he wanted Dora to—no, not see him as Santa Claus—but to think that maybe he had some of the same stuff as the Saint who had worked so hard and risked so much to give others a better life. He wanted Dora to believe in him.

But he knew she was right not to. Nobody else had, why should she? "I'm not Santa Claus. I never was."

She folded her arms, pure defiance. "That's not what you told me in my office the day you recruited me to come here and help you."

He opened his mouth to deny her claim, then realized she was right. Not that he'd ever tell her so. She was right. He was wrong. All wrong.

He shut his eyes for a moment and bowed his head. Not to pray, as he really should have, but to hide. To stall. To give himself a moment to gather his thoughts so that he could say something tender, profound, healing.

"I, uh, you know you're not really fired, right?" he stammered at last. Was that the best he could do? Maybe his family had a point when they ousted him from the office of CEO. "Of course. You know you're not fired because you were volunteering your services but…."

"You don't have to tell me that." She waved away his response then turned and faced the front room. "But I'd appreciate it if you'd share that with your family."

"My family?" For the first time he realized the decorating hadn't been limited to the outdoors. His gaze brushed over pine boughs and ribbons and the little plastic nativity scene his mother had treasured for so long, and the Christmas tree, with a tinfoil star on the top.

"Yes. Please tell your family you did not really just fire me." She frowned, cast her eyes down, then exhaled as if to say *moving on now*. Only she didn't move on. "It may seem like small thing to you but I care what they think of me. And, well, I've never been fired from anything in my life."

"I have." His gaze moved slowly again to that star. A knot tightened in the pit of his stomach. "Let me tell you, it's not fun."

She softened a little then, her shoulders shifted. She ran her delicate fingers through the fringes of her dark hair, which now touched her earlobes and fell over her eyebrows. "A lot of really powerful and successful people have been."

"Fun?"

She smiled, though not a cheerful or genuinely amused smile. "Fired."

"Oh, yeah. Yeah. You hear that all the time but when it's happening to you it's not as inspiring as people think it will be." He tore his gaze from the tree, whisked it back over the room, then shut his eyes and rubbed his temple in defeat. "Maybe it's because for every person who rebuilds and goes on to bigger and better things after a failure there are a lot who don't ever rebound wholly."

"Being fired is not necessarily a sign of failure."

Eyes still tightly shut, he rubbed the bridge of his nose, his forehead, as if somehow he could erase the whole scene from his mind. "Says the women who does not want any one in my family to think it had happened to her."

"Just tell them at some point, okay? I won't stick around for it. I should have left already so you could get back to—"

"No, Dora." He looked up at last. "There is no going back."

"What?"

He wished he could just leave it at that but he knew she'd find out sooner or later. "I got a job offer when I was in Atlanta, and I think I am going to take it."

"You'll be working in Atlanta?"

"The company is headquartered in Atlanta but they have jobs all over the country. All over the globe, actually."

"You're going to work for Global?" Her expression brightened. Her gestures became lively as she shot off questions without giving him a chance to answer. "In what department?

What's your job title? Do you need me to show you around? Where will you be based?"

He didn't meet her gaze as he answered only her last question, "London."

"London?" She took a moment to process that. "London, England?"

"I don't think they have an office in London, Kentucky." He cocked his head and studied her. She looked different than she had in the coffee shop yesterday. Softer around the edges. Less angles to her. Less, business. "You haven't kept your hair appointment since you've been here."

"I, uh…" She tucked a c-shaped curl behind her ear.

"I like it," he said. "It will go nicely with the ball cap with the, um…" He made a motion with a couple of fingers toward the side of his head. Suddenly he wished he had shown her the picture of him as a kid, pointed hat and all. Too late for that now. Too late for so many things.

"With the elf ears," he finished.

This time her smile came freely. "So, London?"

"Yep."

"They're taking a second-generation

Southern snack-cake business king and sending him to London?"

They weren't sending him. He had made it a stipulation of taking the job that they send him as far away Mt. Knott as possible. "Yeah, their only concern was whether I could learn the language."

She did not laugh at his lame joke. "Isn't that a waste of a resource? You know the market *here*. The tastes of the South. This is where you have street cred."

"Street cred? As a guy who runs a snack-cake bakery? All I have from that is crumb cred." He chuckled with a tinge of bitterness.

"What about your family?" Dora pressed on. "How can you just leave them behind? What about…"

Me.

If she said that one word everything might change and Burke knew it. And so he prayed that she would not say it.

"What about the Christmas project?"

He had entered all of this with a prayer that God prepare him for what lay ahead. He had spent hours in Atlanta going over every step that had led him to this moment. He exhaled trying to shore up the unexpected ache in his heart that came with the reminder, *Careful what you pray for, you might get it.* "That's my concern now, Dora, not yours."

"Then, I *am* fired?"

"No. You've done your part. You're job is finished."

"But I was going to…" She shut her mouth and pressed her lips until they went white. Her eyes grew still and sad. Clearly she knew that what he'd said was true. Her part in all of this was done. "So the foundation—"

"There is no foundation." Again the double meaning of that stung. His own foundation had been kicked out from under him. He and Dora had no foundation for a relationship. He had no intention of turning this yearly whim into an obligation that he would commit to only to find himself unseated by a better man, or woman. "Dora. Give it up. It's over. I am letting you go."

"Letting me…go." She nodded. For a second her eyes shimmered with unshed tears. Then she rallied, raised her chin, squared her shoulders and smiled. "Well, I may not have any experience being fired but being let go? That's old hat to me by now. Everyone I ever cared about has let me go or let go of me. I've survived that, and I suppose I'll survive your doing it, too."

Burke opened his mouth to say something but couldn't find the right words.

Dora did not share this problem. "In fact, I may be the one getting the better end of this deal."

"What?"

"Because I didn't just get something for my trouble, I *gave* something. I'll leave a part of myself here in Mt. Knott, but I'll take a part of it with me, as well. Can you honestly say you will do the same?"

"What are you talking about? I have given practically my whole life to the people here, to the business and well-being of this community."

"But what have you let them give to you?"

"Huh?"

"You ever ask your family why they voted you out and Adam in, Burke?"

"I didn't have to ask. They liked his ideas. The direction he wanted to take things. I made my pitch. He made his. They voted. I was out. That simple."

"I have known your family for a few months and though I learned the most about them these last couple of weeks, you have known them all your life and you don't seem to know them at all."

"Huh?"

"When is anything simple with the Burdetts?"

She had a point.

"They voted you out because your dad never thought you should be there in the first place."

"Yeah. Yeah, that's the story of our lives. Me and Dad always locking horns. I should have figured he was the one who—"

"The one who wanted the best for you," she finished on his behalf.

"What? No. Dora, this, this gentle old frail figure of a man you've seen around here, that is not Conner Burdett. Not the one who raised me and founded the Carolina Crumble Pattie bakery. He was ruthless. He was hard and driven. He was a man of good business."

"A man of good business? Isn't that the way Dickens described Scrooge?"

He opened his mouth to refute it but said instead, "Close enough."

"And you were on your way to being just like him. When all along, your family could see that you should have been more like your mom."

He stared up at the star then at the plastic nativity. He thought of that picture of him helping his mom one Christmas long ago. Of the light system he had worked to perfect to make his mom happy and of the Forgotten Stocking Project she had entrusted to him alone. "Funny, I always thought I should have been more like myself."

"Well, there's something to be said for that." She tipped her head to acknowledge his thinking. "I've spent a lot of my time here trying to figure you out, Burke."

"Surely there were more interesting things to focus on." He shifted his weight, uncomfortable with the idea of Dora's fascination yet curious about what conclusions she had come to—and if she thought him completely beyond all hope.

She moved farther into the room. "I've seen your baby plate, gotten to know your family, gone through your mother's most prized and even private things and yet, I don't think I know you any better now than I did when you showed up in my office the day after Thanksgiving."

"I never planned to—"

"I know. You never planned for me to

know you. But that day, I did. I saw the real man beneath the CEO, beneath the Top Dawg. I saw someone who wanted to make a difference in the world."

He did want to do that, he couldn't deny it. But how could he when he couldn't even make a difference at the Crumble or even in his family home? He focused on the star again.

"But you can't make a difference in a world that you won't fully participate in, that you set yourself above, even if you do it for what you consider all the right reasons."

"Is this lecture for my benefit or yours, Ms. Checks out of the world for the whole month of December and when she is in it, she's in her office, on the road for work or in a coffee shop at all hours doing business on her laptop?"

"Fair enough." She held her hand up. "But there is a difference between the two of us, Burke."

"There are several, actually, but my mama raised me too polite to point them all out." He smiled, hoping to break some of the tension.

She relented and chuckled, quietly. "The difference I was talking about is that we both started this out as people too busy to—"

"Be bothered by hair care?"

She looked up at him in a quick, startled motion then laughed. "You've been to the barber!"

He nodded and ran his fingers through the closely clipped hair along the side of his head. "I've had a little free time lately."

She nodded. "Me too. And I've put it to good use."

"You don't like my haircut?"

"I like it just fine."

"But?"

The single word made her look away, almost as though he had caught her staring at him too long.

"The difference I'm talking about is that during this season, this one Christmas that I will always remember, I have changed."

"How?"

"I guess I did what you said you should do." He shook his head. "I don't know…"

"I took the time to become more like myself."

"Yeah, but when you do that, you become more like, well, somebody pretty terrific. If I would do that, who would I be like?"

"I suppose you should try to be like

someone who is at the very center of Christmas."

"Saint Nicholas?"

"Christ."

"Oh." He hung his head. He should have thought of that. "Is that what has happened for you, Dora? Has your time here strengthened your faith?"

"In ways I hadn't expected, yes. While I was here I gave my time and attention and in return I was given kindness and a glimpse into another way of life." She moved to the tree, touching the tips of the branches so that the lights bounced and set the ornaments sparkling. "And stories. Wonderful stories. Some that touched my heart and others that will have me laughing every time I think of them."

He looked around him. "I know a lot of stories."

"And people. And pie. And memories. I've only been around this town a couple of weeks this time and I've gotten all that." She stood at the far side of the tree so that he could not see her whole face and she looked at him. "And you?"

Yes. You've got me. If you want me. The

problem was, of course, the thing that kept him from blurting that out—nobody wanted him. At least not as he was. And he was too old to change, wasn't he?

"Burke, you complained about people not doing their part for the town. About them not shopping here, not setting up businesses and medical practices here, but this town already had its primary business, yours. Maybe no one ever felt the town was big enough for anything else."

"Hey, it's a Top Dawg's instinct to bark and snarl and chase off any threats to his, um…"

"Top doggishness?"

He grinned.

"Only you are not a dog, Burke. No one here was ever any real threat to your position in the community and in the end, what did all your snarling and snapping get you?"

"Nothing, I guess. But then, I never wanted—"

"Anything from anyone. That's it." She stepped out from behind the tree. Her dark eyes had grown wide and somber but shone with a warmth and kindness that Burke did not know how to take. "I thought for a time you didn't know how to give. Then I thought you didn't know how to share."

"You really thought those things about me?" That hurt even more than saying he'd look bad in a Santa suit. "People think those things about me?"

"No." She shook her head. "People know you are capable of those things and so much more."

"People?" He wanted a definition. He wanted names.

She did not offer them. Instead she turned and moved to the mantel where the plastic manger scene sat. "Everyone talks about this being the season of giving. There's more to it than that, Burke. Giving is nothing if no one is there to receive what is offered. The baby Jesus came for all of us, but for those who turn away and do not accept the gift of salvation, it's just a story. It's a package wrapped in pretty paper that is never opened."

He wasn't sure what she was trying to tell him.

"You have the power to open you life, Burke. To not just give but to welcome what's given to you."

"*What* has been *given* to me, Dora?

Nothing. I worked for everything I have and even so have seen it all taken away from me, from my position at the Crumble to having a chance to decorate the Christmas tree with my own family."

"Burke, that's just not…" She launched into a denial but cut herself short. She stood there, blinking for a moment. She looked down. She shook her head. "Oh, Burke. I never thought of you wanting to help decorate."

"I used to always put the star on top of the tree for my mom. You know, just because I was the oldest, and the tallest, so I had to do it."

"Sure," she said, as if she really bought his premise that he had acted solely from a sense of duty.

"Not that I won't take you words to heart but…."

"Do. Please. Because…"

Because I love you.

That's what he wanted to hear her say. Careful what you pray for, he warned himself.

She had already turned to walk away and as she reached for the doorknob she added, "Merry Christmas, Burke. And happy New Year—in London. Maybe you will finally find what you're looking for there."

old face again around here until the second of January, either."

"I think it's a nice face." She slid the files marked Personal into her briefcase then met his eyes and smiled.

"You all right, Ms. Hoag."

"I'm…" She paused to think about that question for a moment, to really think about it. "I'm better than all right, Zach. And please, we've known each other for so long, please call me Dora."

"Won't that raise some corporate eyebrows? The head of a janitorial service and a big boss lady on a first-name basis?"

"Corporations don't have eyebrows, Zach. They are not human. They don't have faces, which they like because if they did they'd have eyes and have to actually see what they do to people. No facial expressions, either, because they have no emotions. Nothing is personal with them, it's all business." She stood at last. "And I am going out of business."

"No! You? Say it ain't so. Global would never turn loose of a big-time team player like you."

"Global did not turn loose of me, I turned

loose of them." For once she had been the one to let go, to stop trying so hard to win approval, and it felt *wonderful*.

Wonderful and just a little bit scary. Burke had called it though, no turning back. Her time in Mt. Knott with the Burdetts had changed her.

"I recently came to understand I was wasting my gifts and decided I need to do something more meaningful. I don't want to be part of Global's team anymore, Zach. I'm getting in a whole new league."

His neatly clipped silver mustache twitched, hinting that he wanted to break into a broad grin or let out a celebratory whoop. His eyes twinkled. "I know how you feel."

"You do?"

"Yep. Was on the fast track myself for a lot of years. Corner office, stock options, racked up enough frequent flyer miles to jet to the moon and back. Then one day, fffttt."

"Fffttt?'

"Company downsized and I was gone."

"So you became a…" She pointed to the dust rag thrown over his shoulder and the cart waiting in the hall.

"Independent contractor?" He chuckled.

"Well, made sense. I knew offices. I knew what the sixty-hour-a-week crowd expected. Started my own business. Became my own boss. Twenty-three years later, I have a nice home, a thriving business and time to play with my grandkids."

"Sounds great." She sniffled again. "I wish I'd known your story earlier. I know someone who might have benefited from hearing it."

He shrugged. "It's nothing special."

"I disagree, Zach. You're special. So is everyone who puts in a full day of work, does their best and still finds time to make the world around them a little better."

"I do that?"

"You always make me feel better when our paths cross. Oh, that reminds me!" She yanked open a drawer and pulled out a red envelope and handed it to him. "It's a Christmas card. I don't think in all these years I ever gave you one before."

"Why, thank you, Dora, dear." He poked his thumb under the flap.

"Oh, don't open it here—"

Too late.

His eyes went practically buggy at the check

inside the card with the Star of Bethlehem on the front. "Oh, Ms. Hoag, I couldn't…"

"Dora, please."

"Dora, I can't accept—"

"But you have to accept, pal," came a deep masculine voice from the doorway. "It's a gift. Like life. You have to welcome what's given, then it's up to you to make the most of it."

"Burke!" Dora plunked down into her chair with a thud. She hadn't realized she was doing that until the wheels rattled and she suddenly found herself looking up at the two astounded faces of the men standing just inside her office.

"Hello, Dora." He stood there in his suede coat buttoned up to the neck, new jeans and a gray cowboy hat. "Did I come at a bad time?"

"No," she said softly, when what she wanted to say was: It depends on *why* you came.

"I better get back to work." Zach touched the corner of the envelope to his eyebrow in salute. "Thank you, Dora. If I don't see you again, Merry Christmas and my hopes for the very best in the coming New Year."

Burke moved into the office to let Zach out. He tipped his hat.

Zach shot him a warning look then took up

his pushcart again. "He knows if you've been bad or good so be good for goodness' sake! Oh…"

Burke chuckled as he turned around. "You sure it's not a bad time?"

She shut the drawer she had taken Zach's card from and gave her desktop a final scan. "If you'd shown up a few minutes from now, I'd have already left."

"Starting your holiday early?"

"I'm leaving Global." She stood again, this time taking up her briefcase.

"When? Why?"

"When? Now. Why? Because it's long overdue." She came around the desk, trying to look brave and serene when she felt scared and shaky. And more than a little heart-broken. She wanted to demand of him: What are you doing here? Haven't you hurt me enough? Instead she said, "If you like, you can walk with me to the door."

"Maybe we could head over to your favorite coffee shop, then?" He stepped quickly to the coatrack and lifted her long black wool coat from the hook, holding it open as she approached. "You'll want to bundle up. It's turned cold finally."

"I know." She reached out to take the wrap away from him but with one elegant move he slid the sleeve over her outstretched arm.

This brought him so close that she found her face shaded by the brim of his hat, creating a private world where it was just the two of them gazing into each other's eyes.

"They were predicting snow in Mt. Knott when I left this morning. A white Christmas for sure."

"A white Christmas in Mt. Knott? Sounds…" Romantic and lovely and a wrenching reminder of how, despite giving her all, she was going to spend another Christmas all alone.

"I got the sleigh all prepped." He held up the other shoulder of the coat for her.

"Oh." She fidgeted with transferring her briefcase so that she could put her arm through the sleeve.

"Hoping to take it out tomorrow." He helped her with her coat then left his hand on her shoulder.

She couldn't help smiling, just a tiny smile, then she met his eyes again. "Why are you here, Burke? Surely you didn't drive all the way from South Carolina to tell me that you are planning a sleigh ride on Christmas Eve. Who does that?"

"Gonna find out whose naughty and nice," bellowed Zach from a couple of offices away.

Burke laughed and gave a jerk of his head in Zach's direction. "You know who does that."

"So, now you're back to claiming you are Santa Claus?" She fussed with the collar of the coat.

"No." Burke lifted her hair from where it pressed against her neck and arranged it over the back of her collar. "But I am on his team, remember?"

She pursed her lips, not sure of what she would say to that but feeling she had to say something.

Then he produced a small, square photo of himself, in full elf regalia.

"You found it!" Dora took the picture and studied it with sheer delight, her anger and hurt over the man's actions forgotten momentarily.

"You were adorable."

"What do you mean *were*?"

"And your mom was so proud." She ran her fingertip over the image of Maggie Burdett standing off to one side.

"No. My mom was tickled at seeing me like

that. I didn't give her cause to be proud for a long, long time." He took the photo back from Dora's hand. "I plan to change all that now."

Her pulse raced. What was he trying to tell her? "You…what do you…have you selected a…"

"Let's go to the coffee shop. I have a lot to tell you."

"Tell me here." She stepped over and shut the door. "I'm in a hurry."

"You leaving town?"

"No, I have some last-minute Christmas shopping to do."

"Oh?"

"You say that like you don't believe me. What? You don't think I have anyone in the world to give to?"

"I think you give to everyone you know, Dora." He took her hand. "Only some of us were too stubborn to see what amazing gifts you were offering."

"What do you mean *were*?" She threw his own earlier question back at him with a more cautious tone. Okay hopeful. She did not say it cautiously, she said it with hope. Lots and lots of hope.

"I've changed, Dora." He took a deep

breath, then cocked his head and amended, "I'm trying to change. I want to."

"That's something."

He laughed. "I can't do it, though, Dora, without help. I can't do any of the things I want to do, that I feel called to do, without accepting the guidance, the hard work, the…love of a some very good people."

"You're truly blessed, then." She cleared her throat trying to banish the quiver and hoarseness from her voice. "Because you have a lot of good people in your life."

"Yeah." He took her hand. "More than I deserve."

"Burke—"

"Dora, I have a confession. I didn't come all the way to Atlanta to tell you about the sleigh and the snow."

"I thought as much." There was that sliver of hope in her voice again.

"I had to come, you know, to go to the jeweler's and to stop by the accountant's to set a few things up before—" He cut himself off, his expression concerned.

That *hope*. It did her in every time. She clenched her hand around the handle of her briefcase. "Before you take that job in—"

"I'm not taking that job."

"What?"

"London? Are you kidding me? You know what they call Santa Claus in London?"

"Father Christmas."

"Father Christmas!" he said a half beat behind her. Then he laughed. "No thank you. I am definitely not ready to be a father."

She laughed because it was the polite thing to do, and because if she thought about that statement too long, it would haunt her the whole Christmas holiday and beyond.

"'Course that doesn't mean I'm not ready." He reached into his coat pocket and went down on one knee.

"Burke? What are you—"

"Oh." He reached up and whisked the hat off his head. Only to reveal another hat there, a striped one with elf ears.

Dora burst out laughing, at the hat and in the sheer joy of what was happening. Or what she *hoped* was happening.

"Dora, I don't have a ring. The jeweler told me I would be a fool to just go and buy one without accepting some input from you."

"I wouldn't have minded," she said, surprised she could speak at all.

"*Now* you tell me." He frowned and shook his head, sending the tip of his elf hat wobbling.

Dora laughed in earnest then drew in a deep breath. "Um, I think you were about to ask me something?"

"No, I wasn't."

"You weren't?"

"Nope." He pulled a flat velvet box from his pocket. "I was going to *tell* you something."

"Oh." Her joy subsided. She could hardly breathe.

"Dora, I decided who I am going to give the Forgotten Stocking coin to this year." He adjusted his body, shifting the knee he was balanced on. Then he lifted the lid of the box and held it out. "It's you."

"Me?" She stared at the marvelous golden coin which, unlike any she had seen before, was on a slender gold chain. Above the image the words, "We give to others because God first gave Christ to us," and below it, "The Forgotten Stocking Foundation." "Foundation? Burke, do you mean…"

"Yeah. This year I am giving this coin to someone who can set things up so that anyone who wants to can be on the Saint Nicholas team. I have some other coins, too, and I hope you will come back with me to Mt. Knott to distribute them."

"Oh Burke!" She threw her arms around him and hugged him close, asking, "I won't have to wear these ears will I?"

"Not if you don't feel like it." He wrapped her in a tight embrace and laughed. "Oh, and one other thing."

"What?" she pulled away just enough so that she could look into his eyes.

"Will you marry me?"

"Yes! Yes! Yes!" She kissed his cheek, his temple, his jaw, then paused, her lips just inches from his, "On one condition."

Chapter Fifteen

"I can't believe you made me go Christmas shopping before you'd pick out an engagement ring," Burke muttered to his bride-to-be as he hitched the horses up to his very own shiny black sleigh.

It had snowed yesterday and then again this morning. It had stopped an hour earlier but stayed cold enough that they could use the sleigh over the fluffy white covering on the ground.

"How else was I supposed to carry all those gifts?" She settled into the seat, arranging an old family quilt over her legs. "What is the use in marrying a gigantic elf if you cannot use him to haul your Christmas loot?"

"It wasn't *your* loot." He finished up then

checked the time on his cell phone. "I think you bought something for everyone in town."

"Not everyone. Just the people I came across for the project. And the people on the prayer list. And your family. And a few extra things in case I left anyone out."

"Don't forget those gaudy ties for Warren and Jed." He went around to the back of the sleigh where they had stored the gifts they were about to take into town.

"Hey, with those blues and reds and purples and yellows, they can spill virtually any kind of pie Josie makes on those ties and no one will ever know!"

"I wish we'd come up with a way to buy replacement nativity figures." He looked back where his brothers were hard at work loading the best and the least busted-up figures from his mom's long stored-away nativity scene into his truck bed.

"I was so sorry to see what bad shape they were in. We'll work on getting the whole scene completed for next year."

"Don't we have enough to do with starting a charitable foundation, planning a wedding, getting married, going on a honeymoon, extending the honeymoon…"

She laughed shyly.

Her laughter sounded sweeter than bells, even Christmas bells.

"Oh, please, organize, delegate, take charge, we can do all that in a flash and standing on our heads." She snapped her fingers then paused, and rushed to say before he made a questionable joke, "Except the honeymoon, of course."

He cupped his hand beneath her chin and brought his lips to hers.

"Whooo-hooo!"

"I cry foul! They don't even have mistletoe!"

"He sees you when you're smooching…"

Adam, Jason and Cody began to holler and tease.

She kissed his lips lightly again. "You have given me hope again and restored my trust, Burke."

He glanced over his shoulder at the brothers carrying out the last of the statuary to the truck. He raised his hand and pointed. "Nope, not me. Not my job description. Not even within my means. But I do suspect who had a hand in that."

She looked at the Burdett dog pack, minus

the Top Dawg, carefully lowering the figure of the baby Jesus into the truck and wrapping it to keep it safe. They had to add extra padding because so few of the pieces had survived the years intact.

Adam jumped down and shoved the tailgate into place with a wham. "Sure won't be much of a display this year."

"I had no idea that belonged to y'all. Always thought it was owned by the town and, when they stopped setting it up, that it was gone for good." Carol tugged her gloves on as she hurried toward the minivan to ride with Josie and Adam to the Crumble. "Remember how everyone in town used to look forward to visiting it?"

"Noticed none of them fought for it when the council wanted it removed." Jason made one last safety check then strode to the truck cab where he would be entrusted with driving the precious cargo to town behind the sleigh.

"Hey! Mom never gave anyone a chance to fight for it. Just stashed the whole set away and never even told folks we had it. I think that was the wrong way to go about things. This is a town full of good folks who want the best for one another. Mom never let them prove that. None of us Burdetts have had enough faith in our community that they would pitch in and help us do what is good for us all." Burke couldn't believe those words had come out of his mouth. But he believed them and he was going to stick to them. "And I think maybe it's high time we corrected that."

"How we going to do that?" one of the brothers called.

Burke only had to think a moment before he reached down to the floorboard at Dora's feet and raised the elegant burgundy shopping bag from the Atlanta jeweler. It contained six boxed coins with the recognizable logo on them, but no names, as he'd never been able to narrow it down to the most deserving. His plan had been to give them out this evening as he was moved to do so.

And at this moment, he was so moved.

"All of us Burdetts have been so very blessed." He kept the bag aloft as he spoke. "Not just with money and opportunities but also with health and common sense—"

"Don't forget good looks," Jason called out.

Everyone shared a laugh.

"Yeah, with *devastating* good looks,"

Burke embellished. "And with faith and with, though we often take it for granted, the blessing of each other."

"Hear, hear!" Conner bellowed, and each brother and wife and wife-to-be echoed softly in agreement.

"And with the wonderful gift of having known or benefited from the love of an amazing woman—Maggie Burdett."

Conner again raised his hand but he could not speak to lead a cheer. His sons did that for him, with joy and gusto. "Hear, hear!"

"With these blessings comes the responsibility to give to others. We have always given to our community as we were able. It is my proposal, my wish, my *gift* to you that you share our blessings in a way only the Burdetts can in Mt. Knott, this year."

The men shifted in their boots.

The women leaned in, listening.

Adam, Mr. Get-Down-to-Business, was the one who asked, "What is this about?"

Burke told them about their mother's secret and about his decision to start a foundation, then he laid out his own plan, the one inspired by Dora's assessment of him. "Give this coin to someone you trust and ask that they pass it along to the people they think need their Christmas wish answered the most." With that he handed out the coins.

Everyone murmured and oohed and aahed over them as the boxes came open.

Burke took Dora by the hand, gazed out on the newest members of Team Santa and said, "I say, let's give our friends and neighbors the gift of being able to give of themselves."

Chapter Sixteen

After taking a moment to run inside and make some phone calls, Adam and Burke and Jason had led the caravan through town. The truck and minivan had stopped every few houses to pick something up or to explain what they had in mind while Burke and Dora had gone along ahead in the sleigh distributing presents.

The kids loved their toys, even though they were small. And the families in need appreciated the gift baskets of necessities paid for from the Forgotten Stocking Project funds.

"I hope you don't mind I've been showing off my necklace and going on about the plans for the foundation more than I've been talking about our engagement," Dora whispered, snuggling close to Burke as they pulled up in front of Josie's Home Cookin' Kitchen.

"I'm just amazed at how many people always knew the coins were my mom's doing." He made a shushing noise and the horses stilled. He got out first then helped Dora down.

She ran around and picked out the packages for the regulars. Travel mugs for the commuters. Some soft fuzzy slippers for "Bingo Barnes," the mailman with the aching feet. And those ties for Jed and Warren.

Inside they found the counter piled high with cakes, cookies and candy.

"Folks 'round here may not have much, but long as somebody's got the fixin' nobody will go hungry," Jed observed.

Dora had never seen anything like it. "Let's check the prayer list and see if we missed anyone."

But there were no names there this happy day. In their place someone had written simply and in beautiful lettering: Peace.

And everyone who had come in seemed to have added his or her name.

"That's so awesome," Dora had said, then

turning to the man she loved, added quietly, "I wish they hadn't erased the whole board, though, because—"

"Don't worry. I got it." He pulled out his phone and showed her the picture he had taken of the chalk drawing of a shaggy dog wearing a Santa hat. "When I saw it on the prayer list I knew you still had hope for me. I didn't give you hope, Dora, you always had it in you. You always had all this love and trust in you just waiting to give."

Tears welled in her eyes.

He gave her a hug and a kiss on the nose then hustled her off.

By dusk all the gifts had been handed out, the cakes and cookies and candies shared, anyone who wanted to had taken a ride in a genuine open sleigh and the townsfolk began to gather in the parking lot of the Crumble for the big display.

No matter how many new, handcrafted, specially-made, carved or even gilded figures they brought to Mt. Knott for future nativity displays, none of them would ever come near the sheer wonder and joy and beauty the haphazard, disorganized, motley, messed-up jumble of mayhem that was this year's pageant.

Four-H-ers brought live animals. Plastic blow-mold wise men knelt in awe around the original plaster holy family. Plywood palm trees from the high school theater department swayed in snowy gusts alongside a cluster of children from Cody and Carol's church meant to represent an angel choir.

"This has got to be the most ragtag group ever brought together," someone observed.

"Which is as it should be." Cody stepped forward, his hands out. "Because Jesus was born in a come-as-you-are kind of gathering not unlike this one. He was put in an impromptu bed and Mary and Joseph had to make do with what they had, but you and I know, friends, that they were giventhe most precious gift of all."

"Amen," someone shouted.

"The gift of that long-ago night is the gift we share to this day—the hope of eternal life through God's Son, the light of the world." Cody made a signal and Jason pushed a plug into an extension cord and the whole scene lit up.

Everyone oohed and ahhed.

Then someone called out, "What about the Santa coins?"

Chapter Fourteen

"You better not cry, you better not...Ms. Hoag? Are you...are you crying?"

Dora sniffled and began hastily reshuffling files on her desk. "It's the day before Christmas Eve, Zach. I didn't think you'd show for work today." With Christmas falling on a Wednesday this year, the building would be pretty deserted all week long. "Nobody else is."

"That's why I am here, ma'am." He came into her office, leaving his pushcart of cleaning supplies in the hallway. "So nobody else on my crew has to be."

"You're a good employer, Zach."

"Rest assured I'll be out of the building like a reindeer with its tail on fire the minute I finish up my rounds. Won't see my sorry

"Yeah, what happened to them all?" Dora asked, going up on tiptoe and holding up the one she wore around her neck as if anyone in that town didn't know what they were talking about.

"I got one," the young artist called out.

"Me too," called the girl who had lost her mother and her hopes of attending college.

Burke and Dora shared a smile, feeling their own instincts on those grants had been validated until—

"And then I gave mine to the Sykes!" the artist concluded.

"I passed mine along to Mrs. Beck, the lunch lady at the high school," the would-be college-bound girl announced.

"I got one!" someone called.

"Me too!" someone else chimed in.

"Gave it to…" The first voice shouted out what had happened to their coin.

One by one everyone in town who had been given a gold coin told the story of the gift and how they had shared it with someone they thought more in need than themselves.

As far as anyone could tell the tokens were, in fact, still on the move throughout the county, spreading good cheer and hope and allowing everyone who touched them to share in the experience of giving.

"That's the way it is around here," Jed finally summed up. "Got to look out for one another. Always someone worse off than you if you think about it and count your blessings. Merry Christmas, everybody!"

The cheer went out, "Merry Christmas!"

Burke pulled Dora close, her back against his chest.

As they stood there enjoying the sight, she murmured, "You certainly made good on your promise. This is a Christmas I will never forget."

"Just the first of many," he assured her.

And she believed him.

Then someone began humming "Silent Night."

"God meets us where we are," Cody took center stage—well, left of center, for he knew he was not the real star of the evening. "Whether we are in a manger in Bethlehem or a bakery in South Carolina, He says, "Behold! I bring you good tidings of great joy! For unto you is born this day in the city of David a Savior, which is Christ the Lord."

And the crowd began to sing.

The snow began to fall.

And Dora thanked the Lord that she had found a place in the world and that because of the baby in the manger, she had never really been alone at all.

* * * * *

Look for the next Burdett brother story,
SOMEBODY'S HERO,
available in March 2009
from Love Inspired.

Dear Reader,

I hope you enjoy a little glimpse at Mt. Knott, South Carolina, at Christmastime. It's such a blessed time of year that I couldn't resist it as a backdrop for a book. Since I had hinted at the romance for Burke in *Somebody's Baby,* it seemed likely that he would be the next of the wolf pack to find love. So what I felt he needed was something most *unlikely* to add a little fun in the mix. I looked at the grouchiest alpha male of the group and asked myself—who is he the least likely to be compared to? The answer was, of course, Santa Claus. Once I'd gotten him into that pickle, it was great fun to present him with an equally matched mate in Dora, who had so much to give if only somebody would look hard enough to see past her all-business exterior.

Throw in some colorful locals, a small-town atmosphere, a secret cause for my secret "Claus" and the story practically wrote itself. Well, not really, it took a lot of work, but at least I got to listen to Christmas music the whole time!

For that I am grateful (for the judicious use

of headphones on my part, my family is grateful) as I am for each and every one of you. My hope for you all is a blessed season full of hope and wonder and rejoicing in the greatest gift of all, the birth of Jesus.

Annie Jones

QUESTIONS FOR DISCUSSION

1. Burke begins the story feeling alienated and displaced by his own family. He feels he has not lived up to their expectations and they have not lived up to his. Do you think this is a common situation, even among Christian families?

2. Dora feels her upbringing by much older foster parents made her out of step with her peers. Do you think this is a bad thing? Do you think she might have been less driven if she had been raised to be more social?

3. Dora realizes that the man who cleans her office knows her better than almost anyone. Are there people in your life you think you know well just from observing them, or being in close proximity with them, even though you don't often talk?

4. What do you think your office/personal space and work habits tell others about you? Is it an accurate picture?

5. Mt. Knott is portrayed as an idyllic small town, though it certainly has a lot of problems. Is it the kind of place where you would want to live? Why or why not?

6. Burke is having a hard time moving past his mother's death and celebrating her life. How do you think the loss of a parent, even as an adult, changes the life of a child left behind?

7. The Burdett family, prior to the matriarch's death, had many special Christmas traditions. Does your family have traditions that they have kept up for years, perhaps generations? Do you think traditions are important? Why or why not?

8. Burke is charged with deciding who should benefit from a Christmas coin that would help them realize their dreams. There are many programs for the needy at Christmas. Do you participate in any of these? On what grounds do you decide which programs you will support?

9. Burke has trouble dealing with feelings of having let his family down. Do you think his feelings are justified? Can you see his family's reasons for the choices they have made?

10. Dora has reached a point in her life where she cannot go on as she has before. She wants to be more than a high-powered workhorse. Do you think a person who has been as driven and successful as she has can actually reorder and simplify their life?

11. Burke's mother's reaction to having been told she could not put her Nativity set on town land was to stop putting it up altogether. She felt wronged and that more people should have stood up for the cause. This is happening more and more around the country, how do you think Christians should respond?

12. Dora is a woman who has so much to give, and Burke is a man who wants nothing from anyone. In the end she confronts him about the importance of ac-

cepting what others have to offer as a way of allowing them to shine, to grow and to realize their potential. Tell about a time when you were on both sides of the situation, as someone who wanted to give but was refused or accepted (and how that felt) and as someone who accepted what someone offered and how it affected you.

Love Inspired ®
SUSPENSE
RIVETING INSPIRATIONAL ROMANCE

Watch for our new series of
edge-of-your-seat suspense novels.
These contemporary tales
of intrigue and romance
feature Christian characters
facing challenges to their faith...
and their lives!

**Steeple
Hill** ®

Visit:
www.SteepleHill.com

INSPIRATIONAL HISTORICAL ROMANCE

Engaging stories of romance,
adventure and faith,
these novels are set in
various historical periods
from biblical times
to World War II.

NOW AVAILABLE!

Steeple Hill®

For exciting stories that reflect traditional values,
visit:
www.SteepleHill.com